I dedicate this book, first, to Simone Tammetta, you complete my nightmare.

And second, to the MöRK BORG community.

This is a work of fiction. Names, characters, places, and incidents either are the product of the author's imagination or are used fictitiously. Any resemblance to actual persons, living or dead, events, or locales is entirely coincidental.

First Edition
www.madnessheart.press

Whispers of the Dead Saint is an independent production by Madness Heart Games and is not affiliated with Ockult Örtmästare Games or Stockholm Kartell. It is published under the MÖRK BORG Third Party License.

MÖRK BORG is copyright Ockult Örtmästare Games and Stockholm Kartell.

Foreword

You might have heard this before. But I always tell the same stories over and over again.

I had a piece of paper containing the rules for a tabletop role-playing game called GRITTR in my hands. It was supposed to be easy to pick up and start playing in a matter of minutes. While I was waiting in an eight-hour-long queue to make some apple juice, I started my computer and also made some so-called classes for the game. The sun was shining on that fantastic autumn day of 2018. Oh, suddenly the game was two papers. Still not too long for a convention … or rather the pub. Around that time, I also started to dislike the name GRITTR and remembered a solo game I had published somewhere on the internet. It was called MÖRK BORG.

Fast forward a year. The chemical smell of an item proved very hard to burn. Another gray November. A lot more people than the few hundreds we hoped for supported our viciously yellow project. Me and Johan Nohr had previously set our goals quite low and were aiming for a printed book and a small but dedicated underground movement. Upon the official release in March 2020, MÖRK BORG was already a rather persistent, medium-sized monster.

Yeah, we had a great amount of stuff coming in from outside our isolated nerd den. This was terribly inspiring, so much so we created the MÖRK BORG CULT. That was material done by others and curated by us (mainly Johan making illustrations). We couldn't keep this up, though, both of us becoming overwhelmed and exhausted bottle necks. Thus the third party license saw its first light. It is a very open license and at this point we haven't interfered much, maybe not at all. I think there's more than 1500 items created with or without crowdfunding by now. But sure. There's always a bit of worry when you let go of your dog/monster/kid. With MÖRK BORG, I think the biggest issue (apart from paragraphs mentioned in the license) is that things become too bleak and grotesque, and totally lack humor.

With Mr Baltisberger's *Whispers of the Dead Saint*, such worries were soon to become vapor trails in the cloudy sky, as the story of Dödz Bringare hit a perfect spot regarding the true MÖRK BORG's various mood boards. I doubt I will ever be able to write a full novel about that world, so to see this one come to undead life makes me extraordinarily happy.

Pelle Nilsson, November 2022

WHISPERS OF THE DEAD SAINT

A NOVEL SET IN THE DYING WORLD

JOHN BALTISBERGER

I.

"They keep blinking! I'm telling you, they're alive," a man squealed; his voice was a grating whine that sounded like he was asking a question no matter what he was saying.

"No they ain't! Here, I'll prove it!" a second voice, a gruffer, more cruel voice, answered.

There was a whimper of fear, the sounds of someone being manhandled, and then the sickening **thwack** of someone cutting through bone and meat.

The decapitated head rolled across the filthy bricks and into Dödz's eyeline. He recognized the head; it was Lars Ubenhoktar, a piece of scum who had been arrested for filching bread to feed his starving family. The head gaped at him, terror still written across his features. The severed head's eyes blinked unevenly, the lips twitching and trembling. And then it was still.

"I'll be fucked straight!" said the gruffer voice, which Dödz recognized as belonging to

Earwig.

"I told you, see. Grab another one, let's see how long they survive it!" That whiny voice would belong to Shumshak; he was a pissant squirrel of a man who would only step up in his cruelty when backed up by the larger guard.

"Hahaha, okay, yeah, but let's put some silver down on it," Earwig answered.

"Well, I ..." Shumshak stammered; of course, he was trying to weasel out of the possibility of losing any coin, but Earwig was adamant about making the task of cutting off a man's head and seeing how long he survived more interesting.

As they argued, the severed head began to rock, tendrils of black, corrupted blood snaking out of the stump, twitching, and hardening. After a few seconds, the tendrils had become segmented legs, struggling to heave the head up and right itself. The head turned and looked at Dödz, its mouth opening. Too many eyes stared out at Dödz from inside the dead man's head before it hissed and scampered off into the shadows, unseen by the arguing guards. Eventually, the two guards agreed on a wager and began scanning the rows of prison cells, looking for who they thought would survive long enough but not too long.

Dödz lowered his eyes, not wanting to draw

any more attention to himself, as Earwig paused outside his cell.

"Oh, I think this one's hardy for sure," Earwig called over his shoulder. Dödz heard the keys jangling. "Come on now, scum, you used to be a warrior, right? Used to be important? Let's see if you can make me a few silver, eh?"

Dödz considered simply letting them have their sport; after all, what hope was there for a disgraced fool such as himself? But as the big man came closer, ready to drag Dödz out of the cell and remove his head in the name of science and greed, Dödz exploded into action. One hand came up, slamming against Earwig's face. The jelly of his fat cheek rippled as the knuckle cracked his cheek and he fell backwards, Dödz following after him. Within seconds, Dödz had managed to pull Earwig's dagger out of its sheath as the two men wrestled.

He tried to thrust the dagger into the man's stomach but missed. The tussle wasn't silent either; Shumshank was soon standing over them, summoned by the noise, adding his own shouts to the cacophony and trying to pull Dödz off his partner. But Dödz wouldn't be dislodged; he shook Shumshank off, weathered a punch to the head from Earwig, then attempted to bring the knife down. Earwig caught his wrist, arresting the movement. The two men struggled, but Shumshank's steel-toed boot in Dödz's ribs ended the fight as Dödz fell to the side, clutching at his side.

Earwig rose. He was pale, he had almost been killed by one of the scum, but he was whole. "Oh, scum, you just messed up above and beyond your wildest fucking dreams. We was gonna cut your head off, but now, now I'm going to take my time."

Earwig brushed himself off before kicking Dödz in the side of the head, dazing the man. He moved to Dödz's feet, grabbing his leg and pulling it up, dangling the man above the ground. "First, I'll cut your ankles; gonna end any dreams you might have about escaping. Then we'll have fun." He said the word *fun* as though it were a sumptuous steak, savoring every letter as he imagined all the games he would play upon Dödz's skin. Earwig grinned, gaining bravado as he brought the blade to the man's Achilles tendon, intent on stealing his ability to walk forever.

"Earwig! Shumshank!" The voice was sudden and commanding; it sounded as though it was gargled through a throat full of phlegm.

Earwig winced and looked like he was

considering ignoring it and cutting off Dödz's feet.

"Godsdamnit, Earwig, what did I say about executing prisoners without orders to do so?" The voice, one that Dödz did not recognize, did not sound happy, and it was getting louder as its owner approached through the dungeon halls.

Earwig winced and dropped Dödz to the stone floor, sheathing his blade and giving both Dödz and Shumshank a look of warning. Whatever happened, if either of them should make trouble for Earwig, it would be taken out of their hide once the voice's owner left.

"Master Crol," Earwig said, giving a strange mockery of a courtly bow, then gesturing wildly for Shumshank to join him. "We was just dealing with some churlish and seditious beha—"

"Do you know what either of those words mean, Earwig? Or are you just parroting others? Hamfund, find him," Lord Crol snapped.

Dödz lay on his side, watching the two guards trying to make nice with whatever noble was visiting. Someone important, he gathered, from the way Earwig shook in his boots.

"I can help, sire. Who are you looking for?" Earwig asked, glancing nervously towards the pile of mutilated corpses they had stacked in the corner. If they had already executed whoever it was this Master Crol was looking for, they would likely be joining the pile.

"Shut up, Earwig," Crol responded. "Speak when spoken to."

Everyone stood in silence. Somewhere in the dungeon, Dödz could hear the movement of someone—presumably Hamfund—checking each cell and, quieter than that, the tick of Lars's severed head crawling across stone. He stayed silent and still, letting the cool stone floor soothe his bruises, hoping that neither threat would find him. He knew if he caused any problems, Earwig would take it out on him as soon as the lord left. Perhaps with the distraction of Crol, the guards would be too shaken up to continue their game. A small hope, but also the only one he had. He closed his eyes.

After what felt like an eternity, he heard footsteps approach and a soft voice.

"Pardon, sir, would you be Herr Bringare?" it asked.

Surprised to hear his name, Dödz opened an eye. Crouched above him was a squire in court finery. He had a round and gentle face; it was surprising that someone who looked so soft could also have survived long enough to grow old. How someone so gentle could survive long enough to have gray hair was a mystery to

Dödz. He considered ignoring the squire; after all, nothing good came from someone asking your name. But really, was it possible to be in a worse situation?

"Aye," he finally said, his voice a hoarse rasp. He'd been deprived of clean water and food for long enough that his own words felt like razor wire in his throat. Perhaps answering had been a shite idea.

"Here, lord!" Hamfund called. "I found your man!"

"Him?" Earwig cried. "Sire, this worm ain't no worth for you; he's but a trouble maker, pulled a knife on me just now!"

"And why, Earwig, did he do that?" From around the corner of the cell stepped Lord Crol. Crol was a severe looking man, withered and old, pale with piggish eyes set deep in his skull. He wore velvet finery, which must have protected him from the cold, and a foppish powdered wig that gave the impression of two beehives rising from the top of his skull.

"Ain't no cause to it, sire, he just—"

"No cause? Hmm." Crol smiled, his face alight with the cold joy lords got from torturing those beneath them. "Let's ask him, shall we?" Crol turned towards Dödz. "Well, Herr Bringare, why would you try to puncture our dear prison keeper?"

Dödz once again considered his options. "He was going to cut my head off; I wanted to keep it."

"Your head, that is?" Hamfund asked.

"My life."

"Those are usually tied together, Herr Bringare," Crol stated coolly.

"Usually, but not always." Dödz paused. "Your Lordship."

"In these times more than ever." Crol nodded, coming to some decision. "Help him up, Hamfund, and bring him to—" Crol paused, his nose wrinkling as he saw the state Dödz was in. "Clean him up and *then* bring him to the court."

Without further word, Crol turned and strode from the cell, leaving Hamfund to try to gather the injured and confused Dödz and escort him from the prison and his death sentence.

II.

Dödz scrubbed his skin and scraped the grime off his body as Hamfund poured buckets of cold water over his head from a step stool. The cold was invigorating. It felt so refreshing against the bruises, scrapes, and swelling wounds on his body. And the soap … SOAP! Try as he might, Dödz could not remember having ever used soap before. But it was a miracle thing, making the removal of the funk of urine and old sweat an easy act.

Rinsing away the residue with one last bucket of water, Hamfund then offered Dödz a set of clothing. It didn't fit perfectly, but it was better than the torn and soiled garments he had been wearing.

The two men didn't speak through any of this. Hamfund watched as Dödz cleaned and dressed in silence. Dödz had many questions but assumed Hamfund wouldn't have the answers he needed; he was really as much a prisoner as any of them. Or at least, that's what Dödz assumed about the life of a squire and manservant. Hamfund, for his part, had seemed perfectly content pouring water on a nude man. He made no comment on the myriad of scars on Dödz's body or about the way the clothes seemed comically large draped over his athletic frame.

Once he was fully dressed in the clean clothes that felt like a luxury unlike any he could remember, Dödz was led through the halls of the castle and into a large court. There were courtesans and knights lining the walls, each gossiping and snickering. This, Dödz was used to; it was a scene he was familiar enough with. He walked with as much grace as a man wearing clothes two sizes too big could and approached Lord Crol, who was sitting in what could only be called a ridiculously sized throne. Ridiculous because, if Dödz's memory served, Crol was only a minor lord, a governor of the borough of Hjortkukstad.

Dödz stopped several meters away from Crol's throne and stood, waiting to be acknowledged. As he waited, Hamfund placed a small stool next to Dödz, and a glass of clean water on the stool. Dödz knew he should wait for permission, or at least acknowledgment, but couldn't resist. He grabbed the water and gulped it down greedily. He heard the chuckles and twitters of amusement from the assembled nobles and sycophants, but he didn't care.

"You almost look presentable, though I would loathe to have you in my presence for more time than is absolutely necessary," Crol announced, his voice raised just enough to cut through the ambient sounds of the leeches of the court. His voice was cold and cruel, a void developed over years of being pampered and heeded, of toying with the lives of people he found to be ... less than.

Dödz held his tongue, merely waiting for the haughty lord to continue.

Seeing that Dödz was not going to rise to his bait, Crol continued. "Herr Bringare, you have a reputation, don't you?"

"Depends," Dödz answered. "Depends on if you're looking for me, or my father, or my brother. Each of us have something of a reputation, though each of us are our own. I would not want to be known by theirs nor they known by mine. You'll need to be more clear as of which Bringare you are hoping to deal with."

"No one, least of all this court, enjoys dealing with an ass, Herr Bringare. You are Dödz, son of Owell, slayer of the damned and dead, stalker of the unfortunate dead. Are you not?" another man spat as he approached. He had the air of one who fancied himself a vizier or wise man, likely both.

"And if I were not?"

"Then you would be returned to the prison and to the games that we interrupted when fetching you," Crol responded, waving his attendant wise man away.

"I am Dödz," Dödz stated in response to the implicit threat. He didn't like this; nothing good would come of a noble, especially a petty governor, seeking him out. But he liked the idea of being returned to Earwig's tender mercy even less.

"Good boy," Crol said, as though Dödz were a petulant hound. "This is your lucky day, Herr Bringare."

The crowd around him snickered, hiding their makeup-caked faces behind hands and fans, playing at being demure. It didn't fool Dödz; he recognized jackals for what they were.

Crol ignored them as well. "I have received a missive from my wife. She has asked that I send all manner of comforts, riches, and baubles to her by carriage."

"I'm not really one for family squabbles or relationship issues, Lord," Dödz offered.

"My wife has been dead for months, Herr Bringare, struck down by a sickness of the blood. You see where you come in now?"

"It sounds as though some fool is attempting to play at your heart strings and take advantage, Lord. I feel you need a guardsman or knight to right this. Unless ... do you believe your wife to truly be risen from the dead?" Dödz asked.

"I made the same assumption," Crol admitted. "I sent guards to check on her grave, three of them, in fact. The only one who made it back raved about grasping hands in the dark. Perhaps this is all a trick, perhaps it is not. But either way, I need it taken care of."

Dödz stood unmoving, a small frown drawn across his hard, craggy face. He didn't like any of this, but he liked being executed for the crime of public drunkenness less. He had stayed with his eyes down so far, keeping his gaze to the floor; he had learned nobles very rarely appreciated eye contact. But now he raised his eyes to Crol. The man looked every bit as cruel and cold as when Dödz had first seen him, but there was a desperation there as well, nestled in his piggy gaze.

"I am not cheap," Dödz finally said.

"Is your life?" growled the vizier, the threat clear.

"Stop." Crol nodded. "You aren't cheap. You'll be paid; you'll be paid in your freedom, of course. But you also need wealth. Let us say ... one hundred silver. One hundred silver for the corpse of my wife or proof of her continued state of death."

Dödz considered this. It was an astounding amount of wealth. On the other hand, how much was Crol saving by hiring a hunter instead of paying the demands of his dead wife? Dödz decided not to be greedy, or at least not greedier. Instead, he nodded.

"You have yourself a deal, Lord."

Crol nodded, and a moment later, Hamfund reappeared from some side room carrying a bundle. He recognized the bulky and awkward shape of his lantern shield underneath the cloth. That would be his belongings then, those few meager possessions taken from him when he had been arrested. He accepted the bundle from the squire with a nod.

"What all do you require for your task?" Crol asked. "Ask, and Hamfund will see you stocked and outfitted."

"A horse," Dödz responded, "some coin for expenses, and I'll need the locations, both of your wife's grave and of where the letter said to deliver this ransom that is being demanded."

Now that he was hired, he stood straighter, more confident. Let the world be filled with gossiping, tittering courtesans and eunuchs. Dödz was a Ghoul-Slayer, and a damn good one at that.

III.

Dödz stood in the stables, staring at the horse Crol had decided to give him for the task at hand. It wasn't the worst horse he had ever laid eyes on, but neither was it a very good horse. He could make it work. What he was less sure of was his new companions.

Standing a few feet away were four individuals.

Sohl stood closest to Dödz, a huge man with a large sword slung across his back. He was as ugly as could be. His face was a map of ugly scars, and he had jagged, broken teeth jutting from his mouth. He had the look of a soldier who had fought in one too many campaigns.

Sori was a woman, or at least Dödz thought she was. It was impossible to tell for certain what was beneath the piles of ragged cloaks and little leather satchels tied around her body. She looked like an alchemist, and the smell of dangerous chemicals and rotting materials only confirmed it.

Prongo was dressed like a jester, like a two-meter-tall jester who had spent a stint telling jokes behind the counter of a butcher shop. His eyes were empty of emotion, his yellowing teeth on constant display behind his wide, vacant smile. A range of daggers, all filthy, hung from a belt at his waist.

Io was the only member of the entourage who seemed normal. She was a head shorter than Dödz and dressed in sensible leather armor. She had a crossbow strapped across her back and a quiver of bolts at her hips. Her dark hair and eyes were starkly contrasted by her pale complexion.

They were members of Crol's guard. Or at least, that's how Hamfund had introduced them. They were in fact mercenaries or adventurers for hire. He recognized the sight of expendable lives. Guards were always nervous about leaving their towns; they had families, homes, friends. Even in the Dying Lands, this meant something. These four had no discernible love for the town. They were as eager to go as anything. They also looked to share the camaraderie of a group that came together by choice, not one thrown together by work.

Sohl turned from the horses his team was

saddling and nodded at Dödz. "Well, now that the nobles and riff raff gone away, let me explain how things is working."

Dödz looked up from the task of preparing his horse, watching Sohl's lips to try to make sense of his tooth-garbled speech.

Seeing that he had Dödz's attention, the soldier continued. "The four of us are to get you to your destinations alive and ensure you don't run off with the Lord's money and belongings, job undone."

Dödz nodded, but Dödz was not stupid. The pay for these mercenaries was probably cheaper than that offered to Dödz to accomplish his mission. Once Dödz had dealt with the dead, these four would deal with his life, deliver Crol his due for a fraction of the price that Dödz had been promised. This was the way of the world. But it was easy to deal with; if they thought he would be as easy to kill as any other man, they were sorely mistaken.

"That's the score then," Io said, her voice a soft, growling whisper. "You stay alive and do the job, we get home, and we all enjoy Crol's lack of understanding of how much coin is worth."

Prongo prodded Io, bending nearly in half to whisper in her ear, then stood up and smiled—too wide—at Dödz.

Io nodded. "Prongo wants you to know that if you even think of abandoning us, running off, or betraying us, that he doesn't think Lord Crol is all that picky about how many pieces of you come back." Io glanced up at the jester, seemingly unbothered by him—maybe she wasn't so normal after all.

Dödz looked at his four companions. Even if they ended up trying to kill him, it would be good to have other targets for his quarry. Perhaps once they were on the road, the four of them would calm down and slip into something resembling decent company—although, glancing at Prongo again, Dödz had his doubts. He turned away from them; for the moment he was safe, and only diligent vigilance and preparation would ensure he stayed that way. He began securing his lantern shield to the saddle.

"That's an unusual weapon," Io said, stepping up beside him. "How does it work?"

Dödz considered ignoring her but saw no harm in the question. He took the weapon down and turned it around for her to see. "On the back of the shield is a vambrace and gauntlet, which is actually attached to the shield. A sword blade is fixed to the top of the fist of the gauntlet, but both leave my hand free. This recess here," he lifted the leather strips that hid the lantern compartment, "holds a small lantern. I can use it to see while covering the back so it does not interfere with my own vision."

"Isn't having a flame and oil attached to something that your enemies will attack an issue?" she asked.

Dödz nodded. "It would be, were I fighting men. The dead tend to avoid the flame at all costs. But I am able to snuff the flame quickly when needed, or simply not use it." The weapon *was* an odd one, designed for night raids and dastardly deeds. Dödz had originally learned to use it while serving as a scout in Grift's militia and had grown fond of it. He couldn't count the number of times the buckler and having his hands free had saved his life.

Of course, he didn't rely on it alone; he wore a hand axe at his hip in plain sight of everyone who might think him an easy target with his lantern shield stowed. He also had a few other weapons stashed across his person—a dagger in his boot, a garrote wire hidden in the lining of his pants, and a sling wrapped around his wrist like a bracelet. Dödz didn't share the existence of any of these with his new compatriots; after all, a man needed his contingency plans.

"My dad always said a man with a fancy weapon is a man without a scrap o' fight in 'im,"

Sohl said as he pulled himself onto his horse. "Let's hope he were wrong and you ain't just a liability, ghoul-slayer."

The others chuckled as they mounted and began heading out of the stables.

"I suppose we'll find out soon enough, eh, Prongo?" Sori asked.

Prongo didn't ride any horse—too tall, Dödz assumed. He didn't respond, merely stared at Dödz for a long moment, that terrible smile on his face, then turned and followed the other three with long, loping strides.

Dödz shook his head; perhaps his chances at survival had been better in the prison with Earwig, but it was too late to second-guess his choices now.

IV.

It turned out the Crol family crypts were not as close to the city as Dödz had hoped, and it took most of the day and early evening to reach the site of Lady Crol's burial. Maybe when they had first begun burying Crols there, it had been a lovely spot where the sun shone down and the grass was soft and welcoming.

The sun hadn't made an appearance there in a long time, though. What vegetation did exist was dry and brown, scraggly weeds that stuck into boots and hoof fur as if to cling to whatever life they could, eager to escape the cracked dead earth. The land, like the inhabitants of the tombs and crypts that littered the parched ground, was dead. But that meant very little to Dödz. The dead had ever been unquiet, and as the world spun through the hell that HE had foreseen, it only grew worse.

Dödz touched the pocket of his vest. The small book was snug against his heart, verses of hope and love, a scripture to a god he had never really believed in. But his mother had; she had prayed over her sons as they went out into the world to become whatever they could become in the short time their world had left to live.

And ...

And they all knew it was ending.

Each waking day, they watched the brightening of the sky through the cover of hateful clouds, wondering what new nightmares would be unleashed. He had been prideful then, believing that he alone could train and fight back the ravening horde of undead that rose from the matted dirt, clawing their way across the world like a locust swarm devouring flesh instead of grain. An idealist then, but no longer.

Now he was simply one more mercenary, a hunter for hire. Another drunk seeking to take a life in order to buy his next pint. He stood on the edge of the road overlooking the crypts in silence, wondering if anything he had done would have made a difference now that every day could be the last day of any of their lives. This was always the case, but now the Miseries were upon them. Now death was not some distant abstract but something that every man and woman rose in the morning to greet as a constant companion.

"Think you may stop enjoying the sights and get to work there, slayer?" Sohl asked from around his jagged teeth.

Dödz, pulled from his reverie, shrugged. "I'm considering it, but the sun is set, it's more dangerous now."

"Yeah? I thought you hunted the dead, not cowered from it like some shrinking barmaid seeing her first drunk." Sohl's comment drew a chuckle from his compatriots.

"Cowardice and prudence are two different things, Sohl, though they oft appear to be one and the same," Dödz said, turning to face the fanged warrior. "I am a hunter, but I've continued to survive as one by not taking unnecessary risks. Risks like entering what I know to be cursed ground haunted by death in the night, when they are at their strongest and I am blind."

"Prudence," Sohl spat. "I've seen men like you before, all bravery and bluster so long as you have the upper hand, who flee as soon as your victory isn't assured by numbers or your father's coin."

"Father's coin, what little of it there was, belonged to the barkeep and whores of Grift, not me nor any of my siblings. As for fleeing when victory isn't assured ..." Dödz shook his head. "Victory is never assured. Only death is a certainty; I just wish to stave it off for as long as I am able."

Sohl scoffed a little but didn't argue. He turned his yellow eyes to the darkness that seemed to swallow the tombs and crypts of Crol. "Did you hear the report from the guardsmen that Crol sent before?" he asked.

"Grasping hands in the dark?"

"That's what we was told too." Sohl nodded.

"Wonderfully ominous and infuriatingly devoid of useful information, that," Sori whispered harshly as she joined the two men.

"Indeed," both men answered in unison.

Dödz cracked a smile. Maybe these mercenaries weren't so bad. The thought lasted only a moment before the shadow of the hulking clown joined them and banished it.

"So we need a pla—" Dödz was cut off by the sound of a chilling scream ripping through the air.

Sori stepped forward, but Dödz grabbed her shoulder. "Don't! That's a trap. Whatever is out there is trying to lure you in."

The scream tapered off and was replaced by weeping, mewling. The fear in the voice that floated from the shadows was palpable.

Sori seemed indecisive. She put a muck-covered hand on Dödz's and pried his fingers off of her. "I recognize that scream; I recognize those wails!" she whispered, agony plain in her voice, then turned and ran into the darkness.

Sohl tried to catch her but narrowly missed. "Fuck," he growled watching the darkness for a moment.

They all stood in silence, watching the inky blackness, listening to the sounds of running and sobs ... until the sobs turned to laughter and a new scream joined the chorus.

Sohl, Io, and Prongo all ran into the darkness, answering Sori's fear. Dödz stepped back towards his horse, working quickly to retrieve his buckler. No sense in going into the darkness unarmed. He would have preferred to camp outside of the crypts until first light. But now ... even if waited and let the ravenous dead devour the mercenaries, the hunger would be stoked. The monsters wouldn't be content to stay put. Their bloodlust would lead them out of the crypt and to Dödz. Better to tackle the problem when he still had allies.

Normally, Dödz would have stalked into the shadows silently as he could and hunted by sound and smell. But now, the crypt was alive with the sounds of battle. The laughter of the dead and the growls of the living warriors made hunting an impossibility. With a flick of his wrist, Dödz lit a match and lit the lantern, flooding the graveyard with sudden golden light and twisting terrible shadows.

Around the four mercenaries flitted the skeletal shapes of night-stalkers and zombies, each hungry for the flesh of the living. Sohl stood guarding himself with a massive and cruel looking bastard sword above the huddled form of Sori, who seemed to be attempting to find something within her robes. Prongo was soundlessly hissing at the bat-like stalkers and swinging a large war maul at any of the zombies that wandered too close. Io stood with her back to the jester, her crossbow out, trying to take aim and hit the flying stalkers out of the air.

Dödz was almost impressed with the way the mercenaries had kept their shit together, but he didn't have time to admire it. He threw himself into the combat, his own movements adding to the chaotic dance of shadow and light. Pulling his hand axe out, he spun the weapon to strike with the heavy blunt end, crushing one low flying stalker's skull. He used a gravestone as a stepping stool to launch himself into the air and slammed through a second monster's spine. As he landed, bones fell like rain around him.

He rose and blocked the scrabbling claws of a zombie with his buckler before turning the axe in his hand and swinging to cut deep into the thing's throat with a spray of rotting ichor. As the creature fell, Dödz kicked out, pinning its head against a stone grave marker with enough force to pop it like a putrid melon. He spun towards the next threat, the sword blade on his gauntlet catching another hungry dead man in the sternum. He lifted the creature from the ground and threw him as hard as he could away from himself.

Having bought himself a moment, he glanced back to watch Sohl cutting through a line of the clawing horde. His form was clumsy but practiced, like a man who had never had a lesson in his life and instead taught himself to fight on the front lines of war. It was surprisingly effective, at least against the mindless dead. Io and Prongo were also holding their own, the giant clown's reach enough to keep any of the undead from coming close enough to actually harm either of them.

A hiss in his ear told Dödz he had become too distracted by watching his compatriots, and he fell back just before the teeth of a zombie tore into his throat. Close, too close. He kicked out, shattering the zombie's knee and causing it to topple onto him, but his axe was already swinging, biting deep into the thing's jaw and sending teeth and bits of tongue across the ground. He pushed the monster off him and rose just in time to get hit by a stalker; the winged thing wrapped around him and bit at his face.

"In HIS name, I rebuke thee," Dödz hissed through clenched teeth, pulling from the latent power of some divinity that had long abandoned its post. His axe began to glow with a thin silver light. Despite the weakness of the illumination, nearly lost against his lantern shield, the undead recoiled from it, hissing as bone boiled and dripped, melting where the light made contact.

Dödz lifted the glowing weapon high, allowing the light it cast to wash over the graveyard. Zombies and skeletons whimpered and shuffled or flew to the safety of the shadows.

Checking his wounds to make sure none were free flowing, Dödz walked to the other mercenaries. "Check yourselves for bite marks; these things spread diseases like a drunk spills his drink," he said.

"You couldn't have done that sooner?" Io asked, panting.

"Not with any assurance. It won't last long; we need to get out of here," Dödz suggested, eying the way the silverly light was already beginning to wane. "I can keep them at bay long enough for us to—"

He was interrupted by Sori, who began to laugh. It was not a healthy laugh. It was deep and ragged, as though the laugh itself were glass shards cutting her lungs and throat to ribbons on its way out. The blood pouring from her mouth only strengthened the image.

"There is no getting out of here," she said. "Not for you, Dödz."

V.

Sori's voice, already nasally and polluted before, was now a garbled growl sputtered through the blood she should be drowning in. Sohl and the others were backing away from her, a strange parody of the way the undead had retreated from Dödz only seconds earlier. "We see you, Dödz, we see you and know you."

"Sori, what are you going on about?" Io asked.

Dödz transferred the axe to his gauntleted hand as he knelt and searched on the ground for something amongst the scattered debris and holy relics that had done nothing to keep the dead in the ground.

Sori wasn't listening to Io; she screamed again, throwing her head back as her body began to contort unnaturally.

"What in HER name?" Sohl whispered, putting his blade between him and the possessed alchemist.

A rotting black hand thrust itself out of Sori's mouth, extending to the elbow, choking off any further screams. The arm, wrapped in tattered, filthy linen, groped for a moment before finding the woman's shoulder and using it to push itself further out. The alchemist's skin ripped, her lower jaw falling free in a flood of blood and teeth as a shoulder emerged from her throat. The mercenaries watched in horror as this thing, this rotting man, clawed its way free from their friend's flesh.

Within moments, Sori's ruptured and torn skin was nothing but a ragged cloak being worn by the mummified remains of a glowering priest. His dead eyes shone with a malevolent light. He seemed unaffected by the holy light of Dödz's axe. Darkness radiated from the creature as it pushed the last vestiges of what was once a woman from its shoulders and kicked the loose skin away from its feet.

"SHE is not listening," the thing that had emerged from Sori said, its voice issuing from between yellow, cracked teeth. It turned its burning hate-filled gaze from one member of the party to the next. "Two fool-filled parties of fodder sent to the larder by the soon-to-be-late Crol," it rasped. "And the Corpse-Stalker Dödz to join them. Crol grows more desperate as the days pass."

Dödz was painfully aware that as the holy light faded from his axe head, the lesser undead were growing ever closer, ever braver. He was so preoccupied with the encroaching threat that he almost missed the horrible dead man addressing him by name. Almost.

"What do you know of me, creature?" Dödz asked.

"What we know of you is more than you are worth. Soon, you will join us, and you will know as we do. You will serve the Bishop of Kergüs, the Saint of Black Tears, and hunt those you once sought to protect. This is inevitable. Lay down your arms and bare your throats that we may commune in holy death. Then perhaps you will find your noblewoman."

"I think we'll pass on your offer, actually," Dödz said as he rose from his crouch and threw the fist-sized rock he had picked off the ground towards the priest. He hoped his compatriots would react as quickly as they would need to in order to survive, but he was mostly concerned with his own hide.

The rock slammed into the mess of viscera and loose skin that had been Sori with a crunch like breaking glass. There was a moment where the rotting priest looked down, amused by the lackluster effort, then the alchemical formula in the beaker that Dödz had broken suddenly exploded.

Dödz didn't stay to watch and see if the explosion destroyed the priest; he turned and ran. Behind him, the explosion was ripping apart Sori's other alchemical materials and concoctions, creating new explosions and an acidic mist that began spreading through the graveyard. He heard running behind him, a mad scramble, but whether it was Sohl and his mercenaries or the undead at his back, he didn't know.

#

Dödz kept running until he reached the horses they had tied up, or rather, the corpses of the animals. They had been torn apart and partially devoured. Dödz whirled, his eyes wide, his lantern shield held high. Behind him, Io, Prongo, and Sohl were just catching up, panting as they tried to catch their breath, weapons out and searching the shadows alongside Dödz, knowing death was just out of sight and waiting to tear into them or, worse, inhabit them as it had Sori.

The four of them, down from five, held a tight circle facing outward, waiting for the dead to emerge from the gloom to finish them off. But the only thing that emerged were the soft sounds of the natural world—crickets, night fowl, and somewhere in the far distance, something that was almost but not quite a wolf howled.

After several minutes, Dödz relaxed and sheathed his axe, turning to begin scavenging anything that could salvaged from the massacre of the horses.

"What are you doing?" Io hissed at him.

"Seeing what supplies we still have," Dödz answered.

"What if that thing comes for us?"

"Then we would already be facing him, or at least his minions," Dödz said, glancing up as he pulled the bedroll from under the corpse. It was soaked in blood; it would need to be washed before it attracted predators. "The fact that we aren't already being killed makes me think they are trapped in the unhallowed ground of the Crol graveyard, or else they remain for some other reason."

"Then what killed the horses?" Io asked. She had a good question, one that Dödz didn't have an answer for.

"You are very calm for what we just saw," Sohl said, interjecting himself and stepping towards Dödz. "And that thing knew you." There was an implicit threat in his voice, an accusation that, somehow, Dödz was responsible for what had happened.

"You should not rely on the honest words of the dead," Dödz replied.

"They have no reason to lie," Io growled.

"And less reason to be honest," Dödz snapped back. "Sowing doubt is reason enough. These creatures are manipulators, ambush predators; they are not above deceit."

"And you are?" Sohl asked, stepping forward, his grip tight on the massive cruel blade.

Dödz rose smoothly and quickly, so much so that for a second, Sohl thought he was already dead, a dagger in his stomach. But Dödz had just placed a hand on his shoulder—no blade in his gut.

"I am sorry for Sori, for your loss," Dödz whispered, meeting Sohl's eyes. "Truly." He raised his voice, looking over the three mercenaries. "No woman, no person should suffer as she did at their unclean touch. No one deserves such a fate, and that is why I hunt them, to stop others from experiencing the horror that befell Sori."

Sohl adjusted his grip on his sword, the kindness, sorrow, and humanity in Dödz's voice disarming him as surely as a disembowelment would have. The three mercs stood for a moment in silence, coming to terms with the loss of their friend and their powerlessness in that situation.

After several breaths, Sohl stepped back and sheathed his blade across his back. "We should return, report to Crol what happened."

"Crol would have us all thrown in his prison if we came back with no other information than that. He already knew there were monsters at the crypt," Io said.

Dödz nodded. "No, we have to press on, find out the why, what power cursed the land of his family crypts, stole his wife, and now demands his wealth."

Prongo whispered in Io's ear, his dark eyes never leaving Dödz. Io nodded. "We have nowhere to start. We can't go back in there, not even to give Sori a proper burial."

"There's nothing to bury," Dödz responded with a shrug. "But we do know where to go; that monster gave us that much."

Sohl screwed his face up in confusion; he didn't remember anything the monster had said other than the weird camaraderie he had shown towards Dödz. "What do you mean?"

Dödz kicked the corpse of his horse while pulling on the pack underneath, finally dislodging what he was working on. He lifted the heavy fur-lined cloak and showed his companions. "I hope you brought warm clothes; we head for Kergüs."

VI.

Of course, heading to Kergüs was simpler stated than done. Without horses, the four were forced to journey north with what few supplies had survived their conflict with the undead that they could carry on their backs and nothing else. They had come to the eventual agreement that the only way to fulfill their obligation was to head to Kergüs. The monster that had pulled itself out of Sori had mentioned a bishop, and Crol's ransom letter had indicated some backwater village in that icy kingdom as their destination anyway.

"We can't make this trek," Io whispered as she came up beside Dödz. She cast a look back at Sohl and Prongo to make sure they were out of earshot. "Even fully stocked and with horses, it would be dangerous, but as it is, this is suicide. I would rather take my chances with Crol."

Dödz didn't respond at first, keeping his gaze forward as he marched in grim determination.

Io put a hand on his wrist. "I do not want to die, Bringare."

Dödz stopped; her hand was warm, softer than he would have thought. He turned to face her. She was a pretty woman, maybe gorgeous once, before the life of traveling the roadways and constant war had made her hard. She was still beautiful, but it was the beauty of utility. Of a woman who could handle herself, who had faced the abyss and come out the other side with blood on her hands. He had done the same; it left you changed, mentally, spiritually, and physically. She was beautiful, with her dark skin offset with white scars. Her wine-colored hair complimented the dark brown of her eyes perfectly. He watched her lips, full but dry and cracked, as she spoke.

"Sohl may be too proud to admit defeat; are you as hard-headed as he?" she asked.

He could almost picture her smiling, laughing. What would her face look like if she had lived as a person ought to, free from the fear and the hardship of danger? Would her laugh come easily, or had she always been a dour, hard woman? He wondered if those cracked lips would be soft and inviting if not poisoned by pain and dehydration.

He shook his head, banishing the imagined

images from his thoughts. She was a mercenary, one who would kill him should he show any sign of weakness, and she had just lost a friend. The least he could do was give her an answer, give her some semblance of hope and comfort, even if it was just an illusion.

"There are merchant convoys, small towns. I took the coin from the packs last night; we'll be able to resupply somewhere." Dödz pulled his arm away from her, as much to continue walking as to break the brief connection. He didn't need his attention clouded by attraction; he didn't want to be distracted when his life, let alone hers, would be on the line.

He continued walking, not worrying that she had fallen behind, probably to inform the others of what he had said. He had spoken with a confidence he didn't feel. The truth was that towns this way were few and far between and their supplies would be limited. He would prefer to head to Grift or some other city, become lost in the crowd, and forget all of this.

But he couldn't ... that rotting priest had known him, and despite his assurances to Sohl, it made his blood run cold. It was a mystery, and one that seemed too convenient. He had just happened to get arrested in the Berg that Crol controlled, Crol, whose wife just happened to be abducted by undead who seemed to know him? Dödz believed in coincidences, especially shitty ones. The world was too damn mean and cruel for happenstance not to throw a man to the wolves at every turn.

But this was beyond happenstance. He could see the gears turning in the heavens, just beyond the gray clouds that had covered the atmosphere for as long as anyone could remember. Dödz believed with his whole heart that the gods of good things and decency were dead. Dead, dying, or had abandoned the world to some place elsewhere to escape the coming apocalypse that Verhu had spewed into the hearts and souls of the world.

That left things that claimed godhood, like THEM, and those things that watched mortal suffering with laughter in their bloodthirsty throats. This smacked of divine or infernal interference, though Dödz knew of no demonic power he would have pissed off enough to warrant personal attention. He stretched his mind, considering the possibilities that could have led to his current situation.

He was still lost in thought when he saw a wagon heading along the road towards them. He saw horses, and men marching beside the wagon carrying banners bearing a skull with thorny vines growing out of the eyes. It was not a welcoming sight.

Dödz moved to the side of the road, hoping the mercenaries following behind him would also follow his example. He glanced away from the convoy and their banners, and back at his companions. They had indeed moved to the side of the road but were also approaching. Good enough.

"What's going on? Recognize them?" Sohl asked as he approached, his beady, red rimmed eyes on the wagon.

"No," Dödz answered.

And it was true, he didn't recognize the banner, but he recognized the mentality behind it. These were cultists. He had no love for cultists, and as far as Dödz was concerned, all religious people were cultists. He was aware of the weight of the prayer book in his pocket, the hypocrisy of calling on the light of a god he believed to be dead or, worse, actively evil. But they were tools to be used, not served. The prophecies of HE were making things worse.

The bleakness brought about the nihilist in men, the nihilism brought out the debauchery. Cults rose to pleasure, to pain, to never denying an impulse. It wasn't a completely ridiculous concept—you're going to die, the world is ending, might as well enjoy the ride. But it wasn't an idea that Dödz could get behind. Even if it were hopeless, one should fight.

As they came closer, he saw that the wagon was pulled by two horses and flanked by four guards wearing leather skirts. Their skin was split open by wounds that dripped with puss and writhed with maggots that fell from the weeping sores in droves with every step the infected men took. The weapons that caused the foul wounds, leather lashes with bits of glass knotted into the leather, were curled on their hips opposite cruel looking daggers. Both the lashes and the daggers looked well used, coated as they were in dried gore. Behind the wagon was a palanquin riding on the shoulders of four obese nude men. Thin, tarnished silver chains hung from their nipples, genitals, and tongues, each leading up to the emaciated figure on the palanquin.

That man looked almost undead himself. He was wearing a pale open robe that pooled around his skeletal form at his waist. His parchment-like skin, tattooed and pierced with rusting bits of metal, was draped over frail bones. His eyes shone with a feverish light. Dödz made use of his incredible deductive powers and assumed the ghastly figure was the cult's leader, though he wondered if he stylized himself as a priest, prophet, or as a living god.

Dödz had no interest in finding out. He lowered his eyes, avoiding making eye contact with any member of the cult as they came up beside them. He hoped they would pass quickly and peacefully.

Dödz withered inside as he heard Sohl speak.

"Pardon us, good sirs," Sohl's rumble rose over the sound of the horses.

Dödz glared at Sohl, hoping he would catch the look and realize he was on the cusp of a colossal fuck up and shut his jagged-toothed trap. No such luck.

"We were waylaid by misfortune and lost much of our supplies," Sohl continued. "Would you have spare food, or any supplies that we might buy?"

The cult leader rose from his sitting position, stretching out in a way that his frail form made look unnatural. He tugged on the chains, lifting an excited whimper from his tottering conveyance. As he rose, the rest of his retinue came to a halt, staring with dull eyes and excited expressions. Each moment that passed filled Dödz with more anxiety. The man's eyes fell on Dödz, and somewhere in their insidious and cruel depths, there seemed to be some spark of recognition, as though Dödz was a long-lost friend or relative.

"Waylaid, you say," the priest finally said. His face, already terrible to look at, was made more horrendous by the way his paper-thin skin stretched and cracked as he smiled, a look of manic pleasure at what Dödz assumed was agony caused by the iron piercings pulling at his flesh in unnatural ways. It made Dödz's stomach roll. "How unfortunate. Waylaid by bandits, cruel bandits who have no understanding of the world." He gave a small tug on the chains in his hand, causing the fleshy slaves beneath him to jiggle horribly.

The "holy" man leaned back, as though considering how to help the unfortunate travelers, then chortled. "This is indeed your lucky day, my friends, for though you have lost your goods, you have gained something far more precious, something that has been lost to much of the world. In these times of trouble and pain, in these ages of misery and affliction, when the sun refuses to shine and men slip from apathy to cruelty in abject barbarism, there is only one currency worth carrying. Hope."

Through the corner of his eye, Dödz saw Sohl and Io tense. Finally, they were getting through their thick skulls how precarious the situation was.

"And I know what you are asking yourselves now, what question quests just behind quivering lips, begging to be answered. What hope could possibly exist when HE has spewn such prophecies as the Calendar, when Nechrubel lies in wait over every mountain, behind every cloud in a cloud-filled sky? This is not a burdensome question; it is not foolish to ask. But at last, you need not wonder any longer, for I have arrived. I have come to give to you a new promise, a new prophecy." The man smiled so wide that his face ripped, blood trickling from the corners of his mouth.

"Peace and hope through servitude to me."

VII.

The statement hung in the air for several moments. Sohl and his group had apparently never come face to face with a cult leader before—or if they had, it had been in vastly different circumstances. Dödz didn't move, waiting for the cultists to make the first move. Sohl, on the other hand, continued to think he could talk his way out of it.

"I appreciate your offer of letting us join you, but actually, we had hoped to buy supplies and be on our way," he said, taking a step back as the guards began to move forward, their hands already dropping to their blades and lashes. Sohl's hand moved to the sword strapped across his back. "So we'll have to decline."

"Oh …" The mad man's mouth fell into a little O of surprise. "I apologize, my new acolytes, I was not clear. There is no choice."

The four guards moved forward in silence, raising their weapons as they came. Dödz didn't give them a chance to attack first, darting forward and punching with the blade of his gauntlet. The guard twisted to avoid the attack and moaned sensuously as the edge cut into the meat of his shoulder. Dödz grimaced, he hated fighting masochists. Unfortunately, the pleasure from the pain was not enough to distract his opponent, and the guard used the opening Dödz created to swing his own sword, catching Dödz in the side. The blade wasn't sharp enough to slice through the hardened leather plates, but the impact sent Dödz backwards, trying to catch his breath.

Io was falling back and loading her crossbow as Sohl fought two of the guards, using his large sword's superior reach to keep them from approaching. Prongo, on the other hand, was swinging his maul recklessly, wide sweeping blows aimed at crushing the skull of the guard he was fighting. Similar tactics to the ones they had used in the graveyard, but these were not the mindless dead. They could adapt and assess weaknesses.

Dödz could see it right away. One of the two fighting Sohl was backing off. He would circle around to catch Io before she could reload. Her only chance was to get a kill-shot with her first bolt, or else the guard would be at her throat before she could defend herself.

But there was something far worse coming. Dödz saw that, upon his palanquin, the self-proclaimed prophet was unfurling a weathered scroll that seemed to fester with disease.

Then Dödz's attention was pulled back to his own combat as the bleeding, moaning guard struck out with his lash, the barbed ends of the weapon whipping against his face, digging in deep. Dödz cried out as he lashed out blindly with his weapon to gain room. He was bleeding now; blood dripped down his cheek and brow and into his eyes from where the barbs had bitten. He had to defend himself better; he knew the real threat was not from the man he fought but the man who was preparing the unclean scroll above the battlefield.

"He's a wizard!" Dödz shouted to his companions, hoping that would be enough.

It would have to be, the guard wasn't relenting. Dödz brought his shield up to block another strike of the sword and pulled out his axe with his free hand. He twisted, keeping his shield between the sword and his body while narrowly avoiding a follow-up attack with the lash. The cruel barbs whistled past him, narrowly missing, but it gave him the window he needed. Pushing from his hips, he swung back around from his dodge, swinging the hand axe with all of his might.

The guard fell forward as Dödz turned, the resistance of his block gone, and tumbled straight into the slayer's axe swing. This time, it was more than a glancing blow; the blade bit deep into the man's face. It tore through the flesh and caved in the man's cheekbones, crushing teeth and ripping his eye in half. The man's moan turned into a scream as the axe continued its trajectory through his head. Dödz swung through, leaving nothing but tattered skull fragments and quivering gray jelly in his wake. He turned his eyes back towards the palanquin, raising the gore-streaked axe to throw.

It was too late.

"Nine violet sign unknot the storm!" the prophet screeched. He reached out with one hand as the scroll in his other hand emitted a keening scream that tore through the air.

Dödz felt the heat form on his chest a second before it happened. A bolt of lightning blasted from his chest to the outstretched hand of the madman. The pain was incredible, and the concussive force of the unclean magic threw him back, his body numb and shuddering for several seconds before he was able to pull himself off the ground. He had dropped his axe and would have lost his buckler and blade too if not for them being strapped to his arm. He saw that Prongo had likewise been hit, the clown a jumble of too-long limbs trying to regain his footing.

Dödz knew enough to know that magic was a temperamental thing, unpredictable at the best of times. It was possible that attack was all the priest had in him, but Dödz couldn't count on that. There were still three guards standing. Two advanced on Io, who had missed her first shot. She was trying desperately to reload before they reached her. Dödz was torn; should he help the woman or deal with the wizard? Cursing heavily, Dödz stumbled a few steps before regaining his equilibrium and charged towards Io.

Io was bleeding, those lashes were cruel, but the wounds were mostly superficial, designed to hurt and bleed but little else. They were a psychological tool more than a weapon. Knowing that, Dödz doubled over and rammed into the nearest cultist, using the buckler as a battering ram. As he hit the man, he unfurled, twisting his hips and shoulder to launch the thinner man into the second cultist. He didn't look over at Io as he pressed the attack, lashing out with the blade of his gauntlet.

But the attack was sloppy; Dödz was rushing and he knew it. He had to dispatch these cultists before their prophet could unleash another attack. He pulled himself back up and turned to face his two adversaries.

"You are fools. You fight against pleasure and safety. I can show you such experiences gifted to me by the prophet," the cultist on the left mewed. "Pleasures that make your pitiful human existence seem as hollow as—"

He was cut off as Sohl rammed his sword through his back. The tip of the massive jagged blade burst from his chest, showering Dödz and Io with fragments of sternum and lung. The cultist couldn't even get enough air into his ruined chest to scream. Sohl ripped the blade back out, sawing down as he did, nearly bisecting the man. Behind Sohl, the cultist he had been fighting lay in several still-twitching pieces.

Three down, one guard and the madman to go.

Prongo was rising with a wordless roar, a tongueless sound that still conveyed his anger and anguish. The long-limbed clown grabbed his maul off the dirt and took a few long steps towards the final standing guard. The guard's facade of placid peace fell away, replaced by fear. The man had wanted pain, he had wanted experience, but now, with Prongo's maul smashing at him, he knew that he would never experience again.

The cultist brought his sword up to try to block the incoming strike from Prongo, but the blade was smashed up and away, the force of the blow sending the blade out of the man's grip and clattering away across the ground. Before the man could react, Prongo turned, swinging the maul with the full force of his extremely large, ungainly body. The impact made Dödz wince. The sound of bones snapping like twigs and crushed to powder was loud enough to engrave itself on Dödz's brain. The man fairly flew across the road, a crumpled sack of loose skin filled with shards of shattered bones and hemorrhagic bruises that would never settle or heal. The man was dead long before his broken and battered form settled in the dirt, fluids leaking from every orifice of his body.

In the near-silence that followed, the low chanting of filth-fueled words could be heard. Dödz's fingers were still numb from the lightning strike, but he could open and close them. He looked back towards the palanquin; the prophet was readying another scroll, and flies were gathering around him, called to the rancid stain that emanated from the unclean magics.

He couldn't be allowed to cast another spell.

Moving as quickly as his aching legs would let him, Dödz ran towards the caster, unsure if he could make it. Behind him, Sohl was shouting something, but Dödz paid it no heed. Io fired a crossbow bolt, which whizzed past him, just over his shoulder, but it managed to miss the prophet by a handwidth.

The prophet didn't even pause in his mutterings. His voice rose in volume, a terrible wind rising around him as the spell on the scroll began to manifest. Something vile shimmered in the air, the gaze of Nechrubel, bearing down on them in oppressive and consuming hatred. The unholy man stretched out his hands, the scroll floating in the air before him, clouds of black deformed flies swarming around his fingers as he intoned the final words of the terrible spell.

Dödz, in desperation, lashed out at the nearest thing—the obese man who held the palanquin on his shoulders. His blade drew a thin line of blood across the protruding stomach of the man, but worse than that, it caught the chain that attached the man to the prophet. The force of the blow pulled the chain tight and then ripped the flesh holding the rings off the man.

His nipples and a flaccid hunk of meat that had been his genitals lay on the ground, blood pooling out. This elicited a terrified scream from the man, who bucked and squealed wordlessly.

The palanquin rocked as the support panicked. Then the whole thing pitched over, forcing Dödz to leap back as it crushed the injured man-thing's skull under the corner and ripped the chains and bodies of the other three surviving men. The sudden, terrible pain caused them to squeal and collapse, though none of them were killed by the falling structure. The toppling palanquin threw the prophet down to the ground mid-cast.

The man pulled himself up, surprisingly spry for such a frail and ghastly thing, and the rage from his spell being interrupted twisted his visage into a horrible mockery of humanity. "You dare!? I'm going to feed you to my fucking pigs." He gestured at the obese men, who were pulling themselves up, but his attention was caught by something else. There, hanging in the air where he had left it, was the unclean scroll, pulsing with unholy power.

VIII.

As furious as the prophet was at being interrupted, it was obvious that the spell was angrier still. The air around the scroll buzzed with unclean things, and the chanting of some terrible, painful language pulsed through the air from somewhere outside of reality. The droning chant grew louder and louder, forcing Dödz to his knees. But it had a much more severe effect on the nude men whose fleshy and pallid bodies were closest. They writhed in agony as the words infected them, twisting their flesh inside out. Globs of whitish fat and tendrils of muscle were visible as the men were unmade, unraveling into strips that still writhed long after they should have been still.

Tendrils of black smoke made of dust and mites and manifest darkness unfurled from the scroll. A keening roar tore from the giblets that had once been vocal cords. The dead cultists rose on what limbs they still had and pointed bent and broken fingers at the prophet, each one joining his own voice to the discordant scream that scratched across Dödz's brain meat.

The smoke tendrils shot towards the cult leader and pushed into his mouth, his nostrils, even his eyes were violated as the strands of pulsing darkness pushed the orbs aside to penetrate his skull. Within seconds, his body began to swell, splitting at the seams of old wounds and scars, spilling out black millipedes that turned to bite and eat at the flesh from which they had been born. In moments, there was nothing left of the man but a skull, gleaming white and still screaming. The tendrils wrapped around it, lifting it into the air, and pulled it back towards the scroll that still pulsed with terrible power.

With a pop, the skull was pulled into the scroll, the tendrils folding back into the parchment. The force that held the scroll aloft slowly dissipated, and the droning chant subsided as the scroll gently floated to the blood-stained ground, leaving nothing but carnage in its wake.

No one went to retrieve it.

Dödz, Sohl, Io, and Prongo stood in silence, as if waiting for the other demonic foot to drop. When nothing happened for several minutes, Sohl was the first to break the tense silence.

"Well ... that was fucked."

Dödz glanced at the larger man. He wanted to tell him to shut his trap, that if he had just let the caravan pass, none of this would have happened and they wouldn't have risked, life, limb, and soul against a terrifying power. But all he could do was laugh. It felt good to laugh. Laughter and relief from the omnipresent darkness were so rare that this moment seemed holy—even surrounded by death and gore as it was. Io joined in, though her chuckles were more restrained than the laughter of the two men. Only Prongo stood in mute silence, the clown devoid of laughter, his head cocked curiously at the rest of the party.

"Yes." Dödz finally managed to quell his mirth. "Yes, it was." He finally looked over the destruction. The cultists all lay dead, dismembered by blade or spell, but the horses had dutifully stood calmly through the terrible ordeal, which spoke volumes to the horrors they had already witnessed. Dödz moved towards the large beasts lashed to the wagon and slowly lifted a hand to stroke the nearest horse's muzzle. Sohl was walking around the wagon itself.

Two horses was less than ideal, four would have been perfect, but the fact that the wagon was intact was a bonus. With a wagon, they would have transportation into the north and some shelter from the elements. Perhaps they could survive this after all.

The horses were warm, mortal, normal, and looked healthy. Dödz reevaluated his thoughts on the cult. Obviously, they were monstrous and evil, sickened in their desire to inflict and experience pain with everyone they encountered. But any group that kept their animals healthy and happy couldn't be all bad, Dödz thought to himself.

Sohl yelped, breaking Dödz's train of thought. Immediately, the other three brought weapons to bear, rushing to join Sohl by the side of the wagon, where he had opened the door. Inside was a wooden table, bolted to the floor of the wagon. A woman covered in cuts and bruises was chained to the table and secured with heavy locks. Malnourished and sickly, she looked at them with wide, terrified eyes, her screams muffled by the wad of fabric in her mouth.

Io rushed forward and pulled the cloth out of the woman's mouth. The screams, no longer held back by the cloth, reverberated through the wagon.

"No, it's okay. We aren't going to hurt you," Io said, trying to calm the woman.

Dödz didn't trust the situation but didn't stop Io from trying to comfort the prisoner, nor did he try to stop Sohl as he looked for keys, or anything, that could free the woman. He stood back and looked around the wagon.

It was spacious enough, but the table took up most of the room. There was a large chest in one corner, probably filled with supplies, clothes and food and such. But from every wall hung various blades and implements of torture, enough tools for inflicting pain that it was a miracle the entire wagon didn't jingle like a chime in a windstorm. Or maybe it did on the inside. Dödz had the feeling this was the conversion process for the cult. They would kidnap someone and drive them mad, mad enough to serve the wastrel prophet.

They were likely heading back to some lair or stronghold for the cult. He was even more sure that if Sohl hadn't called out to them, they would have passed peacefully. But it was too late for speculation now; the cultists were all dead, and they had the prisoner to deal with.

"It's okay, the men who did this, they're dead, we killed them, you're safe now ..." Io was saying, cradling the poor woman's head in her hands as Sohl finally came back to the table with a keyring and began testing the locks with the myriad of keys, cursing each time one didn't fit.

Dödz watched from a few feet away, not trusting the woman to rise peacefully, not trusting her to be sane.

Eventually, Sohl got her free of the restraints. Io gathered the slight, starving woman into her arms, growling at Prongo to go find the girl some clothes. A few minutes later, the clown ducked back into the wagon with some scraps of cloth he had pulled from dead cultists. The clown leaned over to dress the woman, but Io snatched the cloths away, protectively covering her.

The clown looked confused, but Dödz understood what was happening. Io was substituting this woman for Sori. She could help this woman, save her; she could do for her what they had all failed to do for the alchemist. A misguided hope, nothing would bring Sori back, nothing would make her death meaningful. But there was less to gain by bringing this to Io's attention than there was by just letting her work through her grief in her own way.

Dödz looked away as Io began dressing the woman, turning his attention instead to the rest of the wagon. If they removed the table, and the hazards from the walls, they could use this to travel into Kergüs, maybe even survive long enough to complete their mission. Assuming the world didn't end, maybe Dödz would get the chance to enjoy a pint and freedom once again.

"Sohl, help me remove this thing," Dödz said, getting down on his knees to see how to disassemble the table; no sense in everyone standing around and doing nothing while Io and the prisoner got their bearings.

IX.

The prisoner, it turned out, was named Portia. She was from Galgenbeck and had been traveling along the road with her brothers, hoping to make her way to her parents' village near Graven-tosk, when they had been waylaid by the cult. When asked about her brothers, her weeping began anew. It seemed one of the dead men outside was her younger brother.

He had stabbed their elder brother in the kidneys and given her to the prophet, drooling and lusting, his life-long desire for his sister manifesting in a move to corrupt her and gain the forbidden things he coveted. The only good thing to come of this was he had been killed, jellied by Prongo before he could ever live out his perverse fantasies.

As Io pulled the woman's stories from her lips, Sohl and Dödz worked to get the table dismantled. In the end, Prongo had to rip most of it apart and off the floor. Most of the tools wouldn't be viable for use in actual combat, they were too rusted, small, or dull, and Dödz couldn't see a situation in which they would take a prisoner, not one who could feel pain the way a living person could anyway. So they took down most of the rusted torture tools and threw them out of the wagon—no sense in keeping such sick tools on hand.

Dödz dragged the bodies of the dead over to where the prophet had been consumed. Messy, bloody work. Moving the palanquin bearers was the hardest, their muscle- and viscera-coated bodies slippery and heavy—though less heavy than if their blood had still been on the inside. He carefully avoided the scroll that sat in the middle of the broken platform. It called to him, whispering insidiously, offering him the power to escape this situation, or to dominate it. Domination lay in the words on the scroll. One only had to have the willpower and insight and reverence for power to use it. Dödz had those things, didn't he?

Gritting his teeth, Dödz ignored the thoughts in his head; they weren't his. He gathered everything that belonged to the cult onto the collapsed platform, grabbed one of the torches from the wagon, and started a fire. While scavengers and wolves could tear it all up for all Dödz cared, he didn't need goblins getting their evil little hands on these things, and he didn't need *anyone* getting a hold of that scroll. Even one less unclean scroll in the world made the world just a little bit better, as far as Dödz was concerned.

Back in the wagon, Sohl and Io were arguing.

"You can't ask that of her!" Io was snarling.

"I'm not asking anything of her, Io! I'm telling you that sending her on her way is safer for her." Sohl sounded exhausted. He probably was; they all were.

"Asking her to make her own way back to a city? How? How would she survive that? You tell me," Io spat back.

The woman sat between them, knees curled to her chest. She looked from one to the other, confused and scared. Dödz didn't have to ask, he was sure she wanted to come with them.

"It's better than coming with us to fucking Kergüs to find some gods damned undead monster! She may run into danger on the road—there is that possibility, I won't pretend it doesn't exist—but we head into certain danger, certain death where we go. One more mouth to feed, one more life to protect, every disadvantage we have puts not only her but all of us at a risk!" Sohl said, his tone making it clear that he had already said this several times.

Dödz cleared his throat loud enough to get their attention.

"Without that table, there's room in the wagon for four to sit comfortably, probably two or three to actually stretch out and sleep. We ain't looked through the chests yet, but I figure they have enough supplies for the nine cultists we killed." Portia started weeping again. Dödz ignored her. "Sending her on her own is killing her, Sohl. Don't lie to yourself on that. Now, I don't care. I don't. We can let her be killed by the world; we can kill her ourselves if you're just set on the idea."

Sohl had the decency to look abashed, turning his head away. Io's lips curled back from her teeth like she was about to go for Dödz's throat.

"But," Dödz continued, "it does us no harm keeping her with us. We may all die, but if we live, it's her best chance at survival. I, for one, have seen enough death on this little journey so far. We put it to a vote. All for allowing her to come with us?"

Sohl glared daggers sharper than his broken teeth at Dödz. Dödz ignored the look as he and Io raised their hands.

"Those against?" Io growled, giving Sohl's glare back, dagger for dagger.

Sohl met her glare with a hard look, but it was less glare and more resigned apology as he raised his own hand. All three looked towards Prongo. The clown seemed to contemplate the situation, turning his unnerving gaze between his companions and the prisoner. After what felt like an eternity, the clown took two lumbering steps to stand next to Io, a clear indication of his vote. Sohl spat and stalked out of the wagon, disgusted.

"Io, when you can, you should take position next to me with your crossbow handy," Dödz said before exiting himself.

Time of day was difficult to judge without the sun. He looked up at the murky gray sky. Based on the brightness of the day, matched with the season, they should only have a couple more hours before it became too dark to travel safely. With the wagon, they would have some shelter, some protection. But they would also be a more attractive target for brigands.

Dödz moved to the front of the wagon and climbed up into the driver's seat; there was little to nothing they could do about the threat of brigands until they came across them. "Sohl," he called, hoping the man hadn't gone too far. "We're leaving." Then Dödz began the laborious process of turning the wagon around.

"I think we're making a mistake bringing her with us," Sohl grumbled as he walked beside the driver seat. "You say there's no harm in it, but ain't the girl already seen enough without being subjected to the sort of shit we saw in the graveyard?"

"She'll see shit one way or another, Sohl. The question isn't *should she see it*, it's *should she survive seeing it*. And yes, it could be argued that perhaps it isn't worth going on once the true horrors of the world reveal themselves; perhaps someone who believed in a benevolent god or a heaven might offer that death is a sort of peace."

"You don't think so," Sohl said.

It wasn't a question, but Dödz answered anyway. "No. What good existed in godhood is dead. All that's left is rot and malice. Why stay alive? Why fight? Because it is all we have when the gods actively hate you. You suggest that she would be better dead than tortured by the vision of what happened to your friend. But the truth is, on her own, something just as horrific could happen to her. With no help, no protection, no chance at survival. But it is worse than that, Sohl. You worry about her flesh, already ruined and tortured. Her mind, already broken by the acts done by her brother. The things that would hunt a lone woman on the road may just eat her body, may just use her flesh and leave her corpse discarded on the side of the road. But then her soul goes to whatever hell awaits us after this, whatever terror we are harvested for. If she is lucky … it's oblivion. I do not believe anyone born in this age is lucky, Sohl. Not a goddamn one. So, we keep alive and we keep those we can alive, and we do our damned best to banish the darkness back, not because we can win but because it is all she, or any of us, have."

Dödz didn't bother looking at Sohl, keeping his eyes on the road ahead. They had far to go, farther still if you considered the true destination was freedom from Crol's deadly task.

"That's it, you think? Just carry on until death because death is worse than life?"

"Because life is all we are sure of, Sohl. Priests and philosophers argue about what the after is. But if it were any good, why would the dead rise? If there is anything at all."

"And if you're proven wrong? Why not worship on the chance you're wrong?"

"Because it's a waste of time; the gods are a waste of time. I worry about what I can do and what I have some chance of changing; the gods don't rate on that list. I won't bend my knee to any power who allows the world to die like this, for us to live like this."

"You think humanity deserves better?" Sohl asked, scoffing at the idea.

Dödz shook his head. "We both know it doesn't. But that doesn't mean we shouldn't have it. It's just more proof that there ain't nothing worth worshiping."

Behind them in the distance, the Unclean Scroll screamed as it finally caught fire. Something dark and twisted, a bubbling unreality fueled by malice, pulled itself out of the ink and from the flames.

John Baltisberger

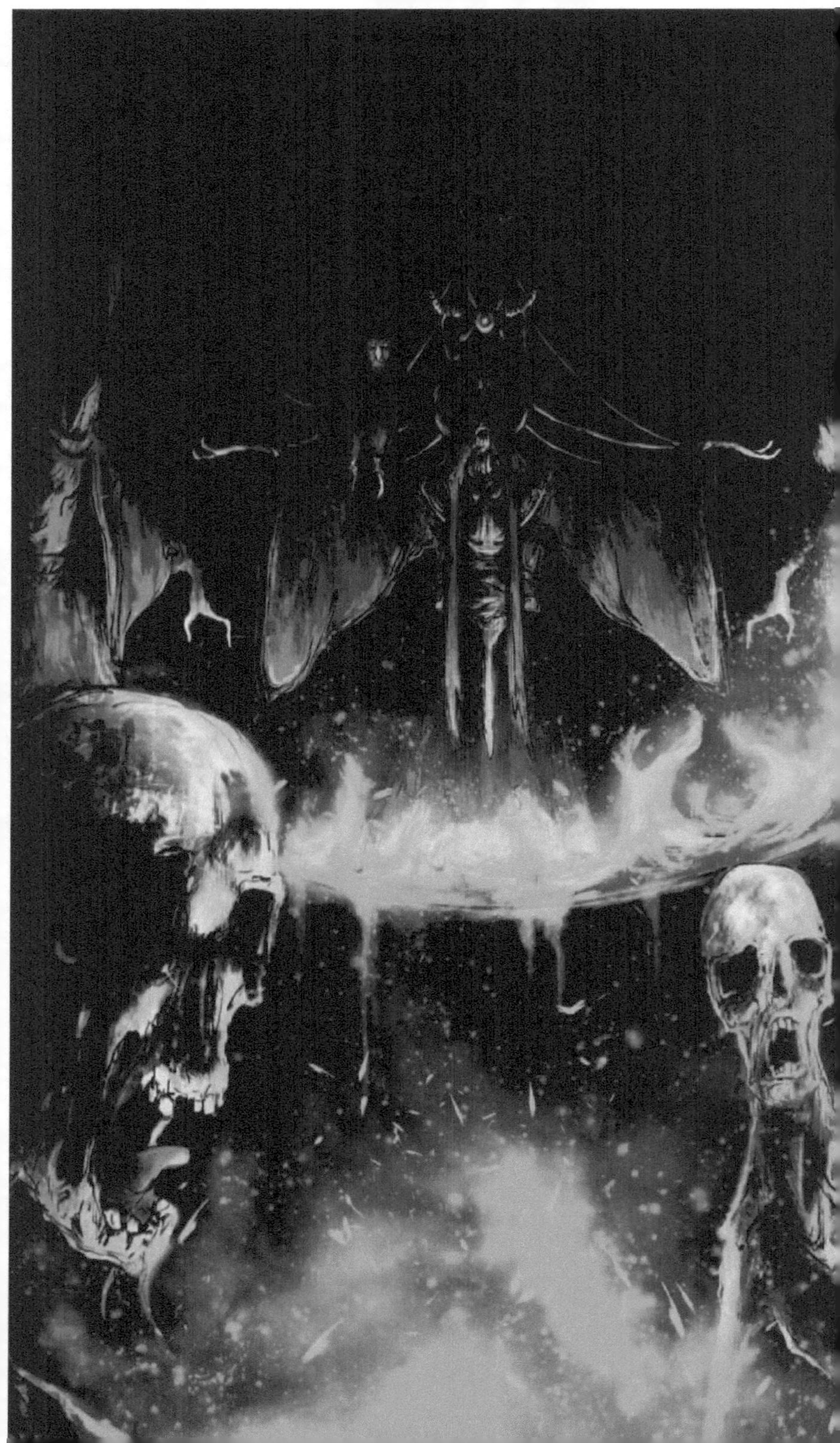

X.

Sohl eventually tired of Dödz's nihilism, or perhaps he didn't enjoy the chill wind that was coming down from the mountains. He mumbled some excuse for leaving and moved inside the wagon. A few minutes later, Io joined Dödz, sitting next to him and setting her crossbow across her lap.

"Thank you," she said, not looking at him. "For what you did back there."

Dödz nodded. "No reason to leave her behind," he said. Leaving her would have caused Io distress, making her less efficient in combat, or at least that was the justification Dödz gave himself. In truth, maybe he was just trying to ease the pain she was experiencing. "Is she safe in there with Sohl?" he asked.

"Of course!" Io snapped, maybe too quickly. "Sohl may be an ass at times, but he is not a bad man. All of us owe him and Prongo our lives. I trust him with mine."

"And with hers." Dödz looked at her for the first time since she had joined him on the seat.

"Yes," she said, her jaw set firmly. Whatever else she was feeling, she did not want Dödz questioning Sohl's character.

He decided to let it be. "Well then, what about Prongo?"

"I trust him too," Io said.

"No, I gathered that, but a man who dresses like a clown, won't speak, and swings a club like the tolling of Armageddon must have a strange story he won't tell."

"Yes." Io laughed at that. "I suppose he won't. He wasn't always that way, a silent clown, I mean. When the troop first brought me in, Sohl was the silent brother, Torn was the talker."

"Torn?" Dödz asked.

"Prongo, his real name is Torn; he's Sohl's brother. But after what happened, he refuses to answer to it, only answers to Prongo now. Anyway, Torn was the jovial one; Sohl was sour and withdrawn. I think it was part of a tough guy act on his part." Io fell silent, her dark eyes scanning the horizon for threats. They had crossed over into Kergüs, where cold snow accrued on the ground, turning the world gray, completely devoid of warmth.

Dödz pulled his cloak a bit tighter around

his shoulders to ward off the chill. "So what happened?"

Io's eyes snapped towards him as if she were coming out of a trance built by her memories. "He mouthed off to the wrong noble; people died." Her tone was about as warm as the air around them. Whatever had happened to their troop, it had left deep scars on all of them.

Part of Dödz wanted to leave it there, allow her the private pain of her memories, but knowing what scars his comrades in arms had would better help him survive. "What people?" he pressed.

Io's lips pulled back in a snarl, though she didn't voice her anger, instead she spoke in a low hushed tone, as though worried Sohl or Prongo would hear her. "We had this job back in the Wästland. We were told it was an escaped prisoner; we were to fetch him, bring him back. Well, we found him, had to fight tooth and nail to extract him from the scum that had rescued him, and then we dragged him back to Schleswig. The entire time, the prisoner was mouthy, rude, demanding. It was pretty clear that he thought he was above us, which, given the circumstances, we found hilarious. Because he had given us so much trouble, and because he was a simple prisoner who we thought we were dragging back to his execution, Torn decided to fill his boredom by mocking the prisoner. And, Dödz, Torn was clever, hilariously clever. Every word the prisoner spoke, Torn had two harsher words back. He talked circles around the man and made him wallow in his own foolishness."

Her eyes got a faraway look. "But it turns out he wasn't a prisoner; he was some nephew of Fathmu. He had been running to avoid marrying some other noble in an arranged marriage. He wanted no part of Schleswig's nobility, not until Torn had made him feel a fool. After that, he was very excited to get back to his family and the power it meant he had. His first act was demanding our troop be rounded up and imprisoned. He forced Torn into the fucking clown costume, called him Prongo. Most of us were tortured and killed in front of him. The entire time, that piece of shit we had rescued cracked jokes, laughing, mocking. His own little revenge." She trailed off.

"How did you all escape?" Dödz asked when it was clear that Io had stopped talking.

"Despite his poor treatment, the little shit would be dead without us. So, Sohl bartered, not with the son but with his father, the duke. He let his son have his fun. For days, we stayed in that prison, enjoying the boy's tender mercies and vengeance, but eventually, they allowed us freedom, when there were only four of us left. Torn was dead, I mean the man he was; now he was just Prongo the clown, and he refused to speak anything other than a whisper or two to those of us who survived. I think part of Sohl died back their too, in that prison. The goodness, the joy. Now we exist to keep existing; we go from job to job. But there's no point, is there? Not when the world is ending and your smile is rotting in a Schleswig prison."

Dödz didn't have an answer, so he stayed silent, thinking about where his own joy had been laid to rest in the dying world.

The world was frozen. Fields and forests gave way to the rocky terrain that would lead eventually to the black spires of Alliáns. The sound of the wind was constant, a howl that chilled the bones beyond what the icy weather caused. A chill that seeped through the clothes and muscles, deep into the brain meat, pulling any warm thoughts and hope out and consigning them to the frozen air.

Dödz pulled the horses to the side of the road and leapt down, leading the beasts to an outcropping of stone that would shield them from the wind for the night.

Sohl stuck his head out of the carriage and joined Dödz as he worked to secure the horses. "Stopping for the night?"

"Have to, too dark, too icy," Dödz responded, conserving his breath for trying to keep warm. Once the horses were secured, Dödz grabbed what little feed he could find in the wagon and brought it out for them. "Between the wagon and the stones, we should be able to get some protection from the cold, but we'll have to take turns on watch."

"I'll take first watch then; you've been driving all day." Sohl sounded almost relieved, likely he wanted freedom from the women in the carriage—he had, after all, been the only one urging them to leave the prisoner on her own to die.

Dödz didn't argue with him. Truth was he was more exhausted than he wanted to admit. Between the fight with the dead of Graven-Tosk and the cultists along the road, he would be sore and battered even without the two days of riding with no sleep.

"Wake me when you grow drowsy then," Dödz said and headed into the carriage.

It was immediately warmer. Though the wooden conveyance couldn't keep out all the cold, it did a fair job of keeping in the warmth of the four people who sat within its confines. A single candle lit the interior, dangerous in a wooden contraption.

Prongo watched him curiously. Dödz understood the man a bit better now; trauma and guilt did weird things to men. Then Prongo rose and pushed through the door to join his brother. Dödz nodded to the prisoner and Io before finding a bit of the floor to lay on. He would have to deal with all of them in the morning, but he would be no good to anyone if he didn't get some rest. No one objected when he reached out and snuffed out the lone candle, and within moments, he drifted off, listening to the cruel howl of the wind through the mountains.

Dödz dreamed of something with long nails pulling itself out of his corpse. Rotting lips spewed holy words in a language that no one living could utter but all could understand.

"And the depths of the underworld shall bring forth flying spectres and crawling beasts. In their passing, the worms grow fat, the vultures wary."

Dödz found himself whole, on his knees before a tribunal of priests in unholy vestments, their skeletal grins plastered across skulls riddled with worm holes. They continued speaking Verhu's blasted prophecy in unison. Dödz rose and stood defiant.

"I know the words of the Basilisk's promise. Each day edging closer to death. Your theatrics don't scare me."

Torches blazed to life with a sickly green flame. All around the revealed cathedral, the pews were filled with the dead. Dödz turned in a tight circle. Each corpse wore a familiar face stretched over a bare skull, pinned in place with rusted nails. It was his own face, repeated unto infinity in that terrible church. They turned, watching him with his own bloodshot eyes.

Above them all, a stained-glass window stretched above the entrance of the cathedral. It depicted a holy man standing over a flock of feral ghouls, blessing them even as they tore his flesh from his bones—a grisly scene dedicated to some black-souled saint.

"We will have dominion, Herr Bringare. We are given the world in icy death and burning damnation." Every mouth opened and moved with the words, spilling maggots and rotting tongues as they pantomimed speech. Teeth clattered to the floor, but the voice only came from altar.

Dödz turned back towards the tribunal. The head priest, a bishop by his garb, was stepping down from his high place, a vulture perched on his shoulder.

"The mistress and the master join in the hollow place. They lead the way to a darkness unseen by all but the blind. And in that place, they open a thousand mouths to wail, drawing the full to empty, draining them of hope."

Dödz's frown deepened. This smacked of prophecy but not of the verses that had been written down by Anuk Schleger. These words were a different blasphemy. The bishop was reading from a scroll, Dödz realized, a scroll that seeped corruption into the air. Even in his dream, the thing was poisoning him. So much evil and malice contained in a single strip of vellum, the scroll itself was a misery, a thing waiting to be unleashed.

Dödz had to destroy it. He reached for a weapon, but as his hand wrapped around the haft of his axe, it froze, ice creeping up his fingers, locking him in the agonizing grip of frostbite. He looked down, watching his skin turn blue and blacken as it died. Looking back up, he saw the bishop suddenly stood directly in front of him, so close that Dödz could smell the stench of rotting meat on the dead man's breath.

"You will not make it, not in time." There

was the sound of a horrifying beast screaming in the distance. The bishop cocked his head, his rictus grin growing as he smiled in horrid joy. "She has found you."

XI.

The wind woke Dödz up with a start. It still howled outside the darkness of the carriage. But there was another quality to it, something intelligent, something hungry. Like a great eagle crying its delight at spotting prey. Dödz threw himself up and out of the wagon; he found Prongo and Sohl sitting around a small fire they had built sometime in the night.

"You fools!" Dödz hissed, rushing over and kicking dirt and snow over the flames, trying as quickly as he could to extinguish the light.

Sohl growled, rising and shoving Dödz back. "Hey! We're trying not to freeze to death. The light will be muted by the rocks; we ain't giving away our position to no one. Calm down."

"The Countess's pets don't hunt by sight, you idiot," Dödz said, pushing Sohl back, causing him to stumble and fall on his ass. Dödz took a step forward, intending to continue his reprimand, when he felt the massive hand of the clown land on his shoulder. He started to turn, but Prongo tightened his grip, squeezing painfully.

Sohl rose, glaring daggers at Dödz and brushing himself off, just visible in the low light of the embers and moon. "The hell is your problem, Dödz?"

Across the night, the screaming howl of the hunter sounded again. Closer. Sohl's eyes went wide as he realized there was something out there.

"You haven't heard the rumors? You haven't seen the corpses?" Dödz asked somewhat cruelly.

Of course, Sohl had been inside the wagon as they traveled. He hadn't seen the bodies of travelers that lined the roadway, drained of all warmth, frozen in horror and pain; the camps situated around frozen, dead fires. But surely he had heard the tales, surely he understood that of all the horrible places in this dread world, Kergüs was the worst.

"Get the horses free; we need to abandon this place."

"You said the roads were too dangerous," Sohl protested, peeling his eyes away from the sky. Snow was beginning to fall faster, thicker; it was getting colder.

"Nothing is more dangerous that staying

here, waiting for her attention." Dödz winced and ducked on instinct as another cry rent the air.

"The fuck was that?" Sohl whispered, ignoring Dödz's statement and reaching for his sword.

"Her hunters, her rangers, her thieves of warmth," Dödz said, resigned.

"Her? Her who?" Sohl growled, growing fed up with the mystery and pessimism of his charge.

Dödz narrowed his eyes as a dark shape became visible in the white flurry of the oncoming blizzard. "Anthelia, the Blood Countess."

The name meant nothing to Sohl or Prongo; they stared at Dödz with blank expressions. Neither of them had ever traveled this far north; and why would they? But due to his chosen vocation—fighting the dead, rime-frozen monsters who fed on warmth and life—Dödz was all too aware of the evil that resided in those distant peaks. He had hoped to avoid any contact with her royal forces but had foolishly assumed the cold men would not seek to thaw their frozen joints by a fire.

The Countess's hunters were among them

faster than Dödz had expected. They wore the shapes of men but were not men, strangely off, like the idea of a man attached to a corpse devoid of any will other than that of its mistress. These were the former knights and suitors who had been drained of life and humanity. Cloaks like tattered wings carried them on the snowy wind.

The first of the frozen knights landed among them with a crash, crouching in the dying embers of the fire, scrabbling among the cinders and shoving the cooling bits of wood into its mouth as though it could save the fleeing heat inside of itself. The remnants of the fire distracted the creature long enough for Dödz to rush forward and slam into the thing, bowling it over.

Sohl came right after him, swinging his gigantic blade overhead to slam down on the shrieking monster. The blade bashed through the beast, its sheer weight crushing whatever internal working the creature had and shearing it in two. The upper half twitched a few times. Bubbling black putrescence leaked from the gaping wounds and froze as it touched the ground.

"That wasn't so bad," Sohl grunted with a smirk. "Maybe you aren't the only hunter here." His smile dropped away as the sound of several more cries tore through the night air.

"Get the horses, hitch the wagon; we have to go!" Dödz screamed over the manifesting howl of a snow storm. He ran to the front of the wagon and grabbed his lantern shield. He didn't dare light it in case it drew more of the frozen knights to their location.

Sohl scurried away, trying to guide the horses to the wagon and hitch them while the beasts panicked at the smell of undeath and cold malice that filled the air.

Dödz watched the sky, hi buckler up, squinting against the blinding white of the blizzard to try and spot the attackers. Behind him, Prongo roared wordlessly. One of the things had already landed and was attacking the large clown. It moved with blinding speed, and lines of red appeared on the clown's body, his clothes ripping as blade-like claws tore at him. Dödz took a step towards the clown, eager to help, before he was bashed over onto his side by another of the frozen knights.

From the ground, Dödz made eye contact with the horrible wraith-like thing. It's ice blue eyes emotionless, its fang-filled mouth lolled open with dumb hunger as it cried like a hawk descending on prey. Dödz brought the blade of his gauntlet up between him and his attacker, trying to scramble to his feet while tending to his defense. As he got to his knees, the creature struck again, smashing against the buckler and numbing Dödz's arm and sending him sprawling again.

They were strong, made too strong by their awful ruler. Dödz scrambled back on his ass, trying to put distance between himself and the undead. Behind it, Prongo was still trying to catch the black blur that was the second knight; his massive arm span made him dangerous, but the thing was just too fast. Dödz growled and tried to remember a spell or blessing, anything that might put these things on a back foot. But the terror of the frozen knight's gaze stole all knowledge and hope from him. He could feel his limbs growing heavier, the deadly touch of ice spreading as the thing devoured his warmth with a glance.

Dödz tried to form the words of a rebuke, tried to focus, but his teeth chattered and his mind slowed. He could see color returning to the dead thing in front of him; it was becoming more alive as Dödz froze. Soon he would be no more than another frozen tableau of death along the road to Alliáns.

There was a twang. A bolt stuck out from the eye socket of the knight. It looked confused, unsure what had happened or how. Dödz was also confused, but the fog that filled his head and the icy grip on his limbs was giving way to warmth once more. He rose from his ass and launched himself at the knight, swinging his buckler to ram the thing back.

He could still feel the terrible cold emanating from the creature even through the shield. He ignored the pain, and drew his arm back and pistoned it forward again, slamming the edge of the shield into the thing's head.

The head slumped inward, caving as its cold, dead flesh broke away and its skull shattered. Dödz flung the now inert corpse to the hard-packed snow, glancing over his shoulder to the carriage. Sohl was hurriedly hitching the last horse. Io stood in the mouth of the carriage loading another bolt; she had saved him, body and soul. He nodded his gratitude. Turning back to Prongo, he saw the clown was faring better than he had been. One knight lay dead at his feet, and he was managing to keep two more at bay by swinging his maul through the air. But they were tireless, and even Dödz could see that the man was losing steam.

"The horses are hitched! Let's go!" Sohl shouted over the din of wind and battle.

Dödz grunted, torn between joining Prongo in his melee against the two knights or jumping on the wagon and saving his own hide. In the end, self-preservation won out. He turned and jumped onto the wagon, turning his eyes towards the sky, terrified he would see more dark shapes descending through the snow-torn night.

"Prongo! Let's go!" Sohl was shouting.

But his brother ignored him, shouting wordlessly up at the swooping knights. He was a whirlwind of violence, the maul cutting through the air. If it were to hit either of his foes, they would be pulverized, utterly destroyed by the force of the blow. But for his life, he could not seem to catch up to the creatures. As he got more exhausted and lost more blood, he was slowing down more, too much. Soon he wouldn't be able to swing that weapon, and he would be torn to pieces by the monsters.

Sohl saw it too.

"Torn!" he called as he leapt down from the driver's seat and charged to join the fray.

Now they would both die. Dödz cursed and got down too. The longer they fought these two, the more likely it was that more of the horrid things would show up. But leaving both brothers behind wasn't an attractive option either. He slipped the garrote from his pants lining and looped the handles through two fingers.

Normally, he would make several loops and saw through the throat of some unsuspecting fool, but he needed as much slack as possible.

Dödz reached the combat. Sohl and Prongo were both blindly sweeping their weapons through the air, hoping to catch something with their swings. Dödz watched for a moment, taking in the swooping movements of the creatures, then threw his hands up, releasing the slack of the garrote like a fisher casting a net into the Endless Sea.

He was nearly jerked off his feet as a ghastly knight flew into the loop of wire. Dödz grunted in pain and exertion as he dug in his heels. The force of his weight coupled with the speed at which the creature had been flying worked together to saw the creature in half. The two parts of it spilled viscous black goo as they tumbled apart and hit the ground. The substance that acted as its blood bubbled and hissed as it hit the ground, quickly freezing solid.

Dödz looked back, expecting that the two brothers would be able to dispatch the last creature on their own. He was wrong. The two men were still trying to fend off the single monster. Dödz readjusted his grip on the garrote, but his fingers were numb, the cold stealing his strength. Stepping forward, he tried to cast his trap again, but the knight swerved, and instead of passing by for a swipe at Sohl as Dödz had expected, the thing landed on Prongo's shoulders.

It wrapped its claws under Prongo's chin and skull and kicked his shoulders with its feet. The flesh of the clown's throat tore, ripping with a sickening sound as the creature wrenched the man's head off his body, trailing bits of spine and gobbets of meat as it leaped back into the air. Prongo's headless body stood for two more seconds before collapsing, spilling his steaming blood across the ground.

XII.

"Torn!" Sohl was screaming his brother's name.

Dödz darted forward, under the grasp of one of the incoming knights, and wrapped his arm around Sohl's shoulders, pulling with all his strength to drag the larger man backwards, away from his brother's corpse.

"Get your hands off me, Bringare! Release me!" Sohl spat, struggling to get free.

"He's gone, Sohl, he's dead." Dödz twisted, using his hip as leverage to turn Sohl and shove him towards the carriage. Behind him, he could hear the knights tearing at the still warm corpse, attracted to the heat of his spilled blood. They could use the man's death to escape, but his rapidly cooling body meant they had only seconds to do so.

Sohl looked like he would argue, like he might actually attack Dödz, but after another second of staring at the ruination of Prongo's body at the hands of the horrible creatures, he took several steps back and nearly fell into the wagon. Dödz didn't hesitate, leaping into the driver's seat and gripping the reins tight as he spurred the horses into a gallop. The carriage lurched as the horses fought the icy ground and the inertia of their burden, but they began to move.

Dödz squinted against the snowy night, trying to follow the road as best he could. The horses were giving in to panic. All their training had seen them through so much terror, but now, between the howling things that flew through the sky, the low visibility, and the icy roads, the beasts were surrendering to their fear and fighting against Dödz's guidance.

He could still hear the creatures behind them. Soon they would finish stealing every bit of heat from the dead man, and they would take flight and come after the carriage. He wished he'd had the foresight to tell Io to get on the roof with her crossbow; at least then he wouldn't die alone.

Die. What a joke. He was here trying to save his life, and for what? He had gotten drunk and not had a place to lay his head. Public drunkenness was a crime? A crime worthy of death? Who the hell wasn't drunk in this day?

The world around them was dying; every man deserved to drown himself in oblivion before his soul was cast into that self-same place.

Instead of the warmth of a bed and a whore, Dödz faced the icy onslaught of the damned and damnable weather. He gritted his teeth so hard he could swear he felt one crack. Despite it all, he realized he was smiling. Sure, it was the smile of a mad man who had lost it all and would soon ride a demon into hell to bargain with a dead god, but it was a smile. Life was pain and hardship, but it was life, it was all he had; and so long as the pain existed, it meant that he breathed, he bled, and he could fight to do so for one more day.

One more day was looking pretty unlikely, though. The road before them was a twisting thing, curving around the swells of foothills and corpses. On either side of the road, cropping up with distressing regularity, were large stakes driven through the ground and topped with decapitated heads of the death. According to tales, the Kergüs practice of decapitating the dead had started as a way to honor Anthelia's penchant for beheading her suitors. Dödz had no idea if that were true or not, but he was mostly grateful for the grisly road markers.

Grateful because he was able to steer

between them as they rose out of the darkness of the snow-filled night, keeping the horses and the carriage on the road. But some of them had not taken to death kindly. Shrieking heads with glowing dead eyes screamed obscenities and hateful slurs at him as he drove the horses at top speed. He imagined that inside the wagon, Sohl, Io, and Portia were bruised and battered by the rough ride. But he didn't dare slow down, he didn't dare calm the beasts. Whatever hurt they endured would be preferable to what the frozen knights of Kergüs would do should they catch them. He wondered if one of the needle-toothed knights had mounted Prongo's head and if it would stay dead. He hoped so. No one deserved to exist in undeath, but being stuck on the side of the road as a screaming warning to others was a particularly grim fate.

His thoughts on the undead road markers, Dödz didn't see the figure in the road until it was too late. The horses bucked, trying to avoid the tall, ghastly figure dressed in tattered and stained holy robes. Unable to turn and maneuver around their hitch and across the icy roads, they slipped and slid, and the carriage tumbled, crashing to its side and throwing Dödz off. The momentum of the carriage carried it and the horses off the road and into the rocky outcroppings off to one side of it. Dödz staggered to his feet, unsteady, hurting.

He rushed to the side of the wagon. There was blood everywhere. The horses had been crushed by the wagon, their mangled forms barely recognizable for all the torn flesh and bone poking through the skin. Dödz turned away from the dead beasts and tore open the door. He saw all three of his companions were still inside the overturned conveyance, though they were in much worse shape than he. But he couldn't let them rest; they had to get out of the wagon and find shelter.

Going down into the wagon, he first roused Sohl. "Get up, come on, we have to go."

"What happened?" Sohl asked, slowly pushing himself up, trying to force himself to stand.

"We crashed," Dödz responded, moving to Io. She lay in a heap; he reached down to touch her shoulder, but by the low light, he could see her neck was all wrong. Her eyes were still open, glimmering in the low light, but there was no light or life behind them. Her mouth hung open, blood dripping from the corner. He tried to comfort himself; she must have died instantly. Of all the possible deaths available in this place, this had to be the least horrific.

He reached forward and closed her eyes before turning to Portia. In the dark, he could just make out her chest rising and falling. He lifted her head gently, rubbing her cheek, and her eyes fluttered open.

"We have to move; we have to go," he said as gently as he could before hooking a hand under her arm and pulling her to her feet. Behind him, he heard Sohl shuffling around in the dark.

"Io?" It was a whisper at first, Sohl discovering her body. "Io!" Now it was more frantic, fraught with fear. "No, no no, not you too. Io, for HIS sake, rise ... please!"

Dödz glanced over at Sohl. The man was losing it. He understood; his brother, his friends, all of his family were now dead for the sake of some noble. "Sohl." Dödz tried to speak gently, to be kind. "We can't do anything for her now."

Sohl looked up, the tears in his eyes visible even in the darkness. "You did this; all of this is your fault," he hissed. "If not for you, she would still live, Torn would still live. Sori ... This is all because of you."

"And if we don't move now, your name will be added to that list," Dödz promised. He turned from Sohl, grabbing his lantern shield from the floor and pulling himself out of the wrecked carriage. He could hear the cries of the frozen knights on the wind but couldn't tell how close they were. He pulled his gaze away from the sky and looked around the crash site for the first time, hoping to find shelter.

Instead, looming out of the snow-flecked blackness of the sky was the silhouette of spires rising from a black cathedral. At first, Dödz was elated; a building, even abandoned, would be shelter from the night, from the cold. They could barricade it, survive the night, and in the morning, as the gray light intruded on the dark, they could salvage what they could and make their escape from Kergüs.

Hearing the other two emerging from the wagon and approaching from behind him, Dödz pushed through his pain and made his way towards the cathedral. It wasn't until he was closer that he stopped, his blood running icy as the frozen ground. Above the doors of the cathedral was the stained-glass window from his dream, its terrifying motif of violent debasement lit from some infernal light inside the building. A tattered faded sign beneath the window marked the building as the Cathedral of Saint Skelvik the Pure.

It was not abandoned, and Dödz had a leaden feeling in his gut that he knew what would be inside. But with the cries of the frozen knights filling the sky behind him, he had no choice.

Swallowing his mounting terror, Dödz pushed open the doors to the cursed cathedral and stepped inside.

XIII.

Dödz walked into his dream. A nightmare of corpses sitting in pews all turned to watch him walk in as though he were the blushing bride at some grand wedding. At the altar stood the three rotting holy men, their robes stained with putrescence and rust-colored rot. All was silence, creating an illusion that this was not an unholy ceremony but rather a tableau. Dödz had the fleeting hope that this was all just a continuation of the nightmare he had been having, that he would wake and look over to see Io sitting calmly with her crossbow. But no, this was the waking world. Reality was the nightmare, and even the most horrific dream was a relief from the truth.

Dödz took a step forward—for what else could he do?

"Ah." The sound was a sigh, like a lover relaxing into the mattress after a rousing session, the exhale of contentment that spoke of a pent-up tension being released at long last. "We welcome the bride of the black-sabbath; we greet the coming of the hollow. We make sacrament in her name." The voice was dry, but it was unmistakable. It was the same voice as from his dream, and more than that, it was the same voice that had emerged from Sori's ruined corpse days ago. It now issued from the mouth of the Bishop, who himself bore a striking resemblance to the martyr being torn apart by the dead in the fresco of glass above the doors. No longer Skelvik the Pure, this horrifying creature before him, this undead saint could only be called profane.

"I've never been described as a bride before, ain't pretty enough," Dödz said as he walked forward, hoping that Sohl would have his back. "You've been hounding us for days, ever since the crypt, trying to stop us from making it this far, I would wager. But we're here now." Dödz spread his arms, gesturing to the rows of corpses and the debased sanctuary around them. "All your plans are for naught."

Expecting some sort of retort or rage from the dead saint, Dödz was brought up short when the thing began to laugh. "Is that truly what you think? Is that what you believe? You insignificant worm! Oh Nechrubel, bless the blind who are incapable of sight, for through them, your works are complete!

"Every step of your path, from your arrest in Galgenbeck to you opening that door, has been orchestrated. We brought you here. We have commanded it. In his name, we played with your fate like a puppeteer, whispering through the dreams and prayers of the insane and faithful to guide you to this place, in this season, at this moment. Praise be Yetsabu-Nech!"

Dödz was at a loss. What possible purpose could this monster have for bringing him here? What part did he have to play in its foul plots? Before he could ask, Portia stepped past him as though she were in a dream. Dödz grabbed for her to stop her from walking towards the unholy priest, but she deftly avoided his grasp, slipping away like mist in the morning dawn.

"Portia, what are you doing?" he asked, watching, horrified, as she ascended the dais and took Skelvik's hand. "Damn you, fiend, lift your spell and face me. Leave her out of your sick rituals."

"Leave her out of my rituals? Shall we ask her?" The terrible dead smile of the bishop turned thoughtful as he angled his head towards Portia. "Well, my Lady Crol, how say you?"

She turned her eyes from Skelvik to Dödz, the facade of demure fear and vulnerability falling away, leaving a face lined in hard, cruel hatred. "He played his part perfectly." Her voice was hollow, like a leaden bell chiming in a great auditorium. It crashed into Dödz's brain, leaving his thoughts muddled and aching and his body feeling empty and useless. How was any of this possible?

"But now," she continued, "he has played out his worth. They all have."

"Indeed," the saint whispered, still terribly audible in the dead silence of the sanctuary. "I am sorry, Herr Bringare, your services are no longer required."

Dödz growled and stepped back, expecting the dead to attack him at any moment. "So long as I still stand, I stand between you and your plans."

The saint tilted his head, the awful smile filled with rotting teeth lining worm-riddled gums returning. "You stand between nothing, Herr Bringare, nothing at all." He turned, still holding Portia's hand, and began leading Lady Crol out through the back.

Dödz took a step forward to give chase when Sohl's voice rang out, distraught and crazed.

"Bringare!" Sohl howled.

Dödz turned and saw the man was half mad, his eyes bloodshot, spittle foaming at his mouth. Behind his shoulder, an image of the saint, ephemeral and unreal, hovered, whispering in his ear.

"You did this! My family is dead because of you!" Sohl didn't wait for Dödz to respond, rushing forward, his sword swinging in wild, angry arcs.

Dödz angled himself to take the brunt of the swing on the shield. The attack cracked the shield, shooting thunder and lightning up his arm in agonizing jolts. Dödz backed up, trying to keep out of the way of those swings. He had seen Sohl fight, and he was skilled, but his anger, frothed to a berserk rage by the specter of the saint, made him reckless.

Dödz maneuvered away from Sohl, diving and rolling under a wild swipe of the sword and into the aisles. The corpses that sat there fell apart, crumbling to frozen moldering dust as he passed. He paid them no mind, trying to unbuckle the ruined buckler from his arm while avoiding the onslaught from his companion.

"Think clearly, Sohl; I caused none of this!" He ran a few steps, putting as many of the pews between them as possible. "I did not assign you to this task, Crol did!"

"The task would not exist without you!" Sohl spat back.

"I did not kill Sori; I did not lead us to that place!" Dödz argued.

"You did not save her either! You are supposed to be some great hunter, and all you do is *fail*!" He screamed the last word, launching himself over the pews at Dödz.

Dödz lifted his sword, but it had been damaged by the blow that cracked the buckler and gave way, allowing Sohl to cut a terrible gash across his shoulder.

Dödz fell back, his sword laying broken on the floor. Crawling backwards, scuttling away from Sohl, he tried again. "I did not kill your brother, Sohl."

The ghastly image of the saint whispered into Sohl's ear again, and the man spoke through gritted teeth. "You brought us here; you might as well have killed him yourself!" Sohl said.

He was beyond reason. Sohl raised his sword, intent on cutting Dödz in half. The massive blade, as deadly as it was, as well as Sohl wielded it, was a slow and clumsy weapon. Dödz rose from his supine position, the dagger from his boot in his hand, and slammed the blade into Sohl's chest, sliding under the ribs and into the lungs.

Despite the blow, Sohl leaned forward and bit

into Dödz injured shoulder, tearing at the flesh. Dödz screamed in pain and pulled away, leaving ragged strips of cloth and flesh stuck in Sohl's teeth. Dödz turned, sliced out with the dagger, and cut through the guard on Sohl's arm, then reversed his grip and cut the other arm. Sohl, losing blood quickly, could not hold on to his blade, and it fell from his numbing fingers.

Still, he spat curses, ambling forward, his mouth working in frantic chomps, so like the undead zombies Dödz had fought in the past. A sane man would know he lost the fight, that his lung was filling with fluid and he would soon choke to death, but Sohl's mind was ruined by the tender ministrations of the saint. He could not be saved.

Dödz ducked under another attack, Sohl's teeth coming within inches of his face. He stepped around the larger man and turned, raising his blade and punching it through Sohl's ear. The blade passed harmlessly through the shade of the saint as it entered Sohl's skull. Blood and brains slid out of his ear as Dödz ripped the dagger back out of his head.

Sohl managed one step before he sank to his knees and then fell forward, dead. The ghostly image of the saint threw back its head, a suddenly audible laughter filling the cathedral.

It was the laughter of victory.

Dödz staggered out of the cathedral to escape the sound of the dead man's laughter and the sight of Sohl's corpse. Outside was no better. The sky was brightening into the gray, bland half-light they were now forced to called day. The light and change in location did not improve matters. During his time in the cathedral, the Countess's terrible knights had found the carriage. They had ripped the horse carcasses to shredded lumps of torn flesh and frozen blood. But worst of all, one had pulled Io's corpse from the wreckage and propped her up naked against a post, her frozen corpse posed to point an accusing finger at the cathedral, and at Dödz, who had just exited.

He turned away from her accusing eyes, muttering an apology, and began to walk.

He had no plan. He was losing blood, and his willpower and exhaustion had reached their limit. He had taken only a few steps before he pitched forward to lie prone in the street. Dödz had just enough strength to be grateful he would be dead before night fell and the frozen knights returned.

Epilogue

Dödz woke up in a warm bed. For a moment, he questioned whether perhaps his dismissal of heaven had been too swift. But then the pain returned. He tried to turn and look around the room but could only tell he was inside.

"Ah, he awakens. See, Mother, I told you he would live!"

A face filled his vision, a young woman. Her face was quickly replaced with a damp cloth that she wiped over his face. The coolness almost made him jump, but it was a relief too. He must have a fever, he realized.

"Too strong to die," the girl was saying.

"Stop fawning over him and get to the kitchen!" another voice chided. The girl frowned but hurried away. Dödz listened to her footsteps retreat and then another, heavier pair come forward. "I'll be damned by SHE if she wasn't truthful, though; didn't expect you to make it." The face that appeared now was older, pretty, and worn. Someone who had lived a hard life but had somehow managed to keep some goodness in her.

"How did I get here?" Dödz croaked.

The woman clucked her tongue and helped Dödz sit up, ignoring his wincing, so he could drink some water from a bowl she had brought.

"You were found in the road on the way from Alliáns. Traders found you, thought you was dead, but as they were going through your pockets, they saw you were still alive, decided to bring you here in case you could reward them upon recovery."

Dödz scoffed but nodded. He would have likely done the same thing. "I'm afraid all my coin was in my carriage. I'm sure they emptied that already."

The woman nodded, though he wasn't sure if she was just agreeing with the sentiment or if the traders had said as much. Dödz thought back to his last memories, to what had happened.

"I was heading to Galgenbeck," he finally said, not the whole truth but enough of one. If his intuition was right, the saint and Lady Crol, Portia, would be heading there themselves. "Or rather, to Extberg, near Galgenbeck."

"Oh." The woman looked taken back. "I, well, you won't be going there now, I don't think."

Dödz quirked an eyebrow, hoping she would elaborate.

"Well, word is that Extberg is gone, the city collapsed. Ain't no one going in there; ain't no one coming out either. Terrible stink rising from the ground where it were. Worse part is it seems to be catching. Cities and towns just emptying out; no one knows where any of the people are going. But I would stay away from Extberg, even Galgenbeck, what with all the worms and vultures and missing people. Only a matter of time 'fore ..."

She kept talking, but Dödz had stopped listening. Instead, he heard in his mind:

The city shall be made hollow. Of those who rest in hollowness, they shall not be seen. And the earth shall shake and be riven. And from the cracks shall rise a poisonous mist, and in ten days, it will shroud the world.

Of those who build mightily, stone by stone, so shall they fall, stone by stone.

The Nameless Scriptures, Psalm 1.1

The Reliquary of St. Skelvik the Profane

7

EVERY HALLWAY is trapped or occupied

4

5

6. The Chamber of Lights

d4 Random Traps

1. A living skull set in a crevice, its screams to attract d3 wraiths.
2. A pressure plate causes spears (d4) to stab from the wall. Test Agility to avoid.
3. The floor falls away into a pit Test d14 agility or take d6 damage.
4. A trail of broken glass. Test d12 presence or alert d2 Undead Dolls

entrance

d4 Random Encounters

1. 1d4 Zombies dressed as pilgrims.
2. a pack d6 of feral Dogs pick over bones
3. The Svered Head of Lars Ubenhoktar skitters towards you.
4. An escaped Wickhead staggers through the shadows, dim and rabid.

2. The Nodhdome

3

Feral Dogs
HP: 4 | Morale 7
Scabby Hide -d2
Dmg: Bite d2

The Severed Head of Lars
HP: 12 | Morale 4
Thick Skull -d2
Dmg: Bite d2
Special: Spit bile: d2 + Poison!

2. The Nodhdome
An arena littered with the rusted weapons and armor all useless. fetid corpses lie strewn about.
A lone berserker battles d20 zombies. She is not friendly.

AINT SKELVIK THE PROFANE
P 30 | Morale - | Magic Barrier -d4 | Claws d2
ecial Whispers of the Dead Saint: The Saint kes control of a player (test Presence d14 to oid, repeat test every turn to break spell) elvik also has access to 3 random unclean scrolls

elvik does not make morale checks, but will sperse into a cloud of plague ash if brought low capeing through the cracks in the walls.

3
cistern with a drain, ood stains all, the eshy remains litter e floor.
blood-drenched eletons hide among e corpses.

The Entrance to the Reliquary is under the abandoned cathedral of St. Skelvik

4
A lich resides here in this ornate yet decayed study. He reads from a book bound in goblin skin. He is friendly and excited for visitors, so long as you discuss scholarly issues....

5
The body of a young woman lies in repose on a bed of flowers.
Eating her corpse will heal any wound.

6. The Chamber of Lights
32 wickheads line the walls dead or dying, barely smoldering. 8 spots are empty. The room is otherwise barren. In the center, a sigil that once held something trapped by light.

7.
This is the burial chamber where Skelvik rose from the dead, a miracle they thought. It is lavish, with all the tarnished gold and rotting satin that a saint deserves, Skelvik waits within his broken coffin. He suffers no intruders.

SLAYER OF THE UNRESTING

Begins with
1d4x10s | D2 Omens |
HP: Toughness+d10

The things that creep in the shadow of night rule when there is no sun to shine. You and yours have ever been rebels, fighting against the tyranny or undead terror that grips these dying lands. Tools, training, nihilism, and, more often than not, debilitating addiction are the means by which you are able to face the horrors that others flee from. You are undeath's doom, until you fall and take your place among their ranks.

ABILITIES

You survive by instinct and reaction time. Roll 3d6+2 for Agility. Close proximity to the damned for so long has deadened your senses. Roll 3d6-2 for Presence. Roll d6 for weapons and d2 for armor. Begin with one piece of gear or a gift.

GEAR & GIFTS

1) The Lantern Shield: A gauntlet, a sword, a buckle and a lantern all in one. Provides -d2 armor, or blocks one strike completely and is destroyed. Can be used as a dagger (d2), and provide light when lit. If used to block when lit, lights both attacker and defender on fire.

2) Nihlus Nosferat: A whip that seems to thirst for the blood of vampires and parasites. 1d2 (1d4+2 to any blood drinker)

3) Unclean Blood: Anything that bites you has another thing coming, You've drank so many foul things and poisoned your body so much that you're toxic even to the dead. You are immune to disease, natural and supernatural.

4) Scholar of Belnades: Knowledge is power, and power is the only thing that can destroy the damned. You have 2 random clean scrolls.

5) One of Us: You have a secret. You fell long ago, you fight to control yourself, your hunger. You live in fear for the day you meet the lich that can control you, but until then, you can automatically sense when the undead are near . . . though they can also sense you.

6) True Faith: Somehow, you have maintained a belief in something good, something that cares. And in gratitude for your belief, you have been given a modicum of protection, -d2 against magical attacks.

LEGACY—MOTTO

1) Bringare—A family of mean drunks and lost souls. The Bringare name brings nothing but sorrow. "Fight as dirty as the grave"

2) Hellsingr—You didn't want to pursue this line of work, but it comes to find you. "Know thine enemy and end them in the shadows"

3) Morris—Your family has always served other hunters, working with no glory of your own. "When they fall we shall rise".

4) Summers—One of you will be the Chosen One, it's just a matter of not letting the line die off before then. "The hardest thing in this world is to live in it."

5) Belmont—Generation after generation sacrificed to the fight, when will it end, when will the dead finally stay down? "A man is nothing more than a miserable pile of secrets."

6) Skelvik—Your family name has forever been cursed by what should have been your most blessed ancestor. You hunt not for justice, but for redemption. "Only in the darkest places may the brightest shine."

John Baltisberger

John Baltisberger is an award-winning author of speculative and genre fiction that often focuses on Jewish Elements. Beyond his writing career, John is a game designer and the Publishing Editor of Madness Heart Press, Madness Heart Games, and Aggadah Try It.

A fan of transgressive and experimental literature. He lives with his wife, daughter and trash-goblin/pug Beans in Austin, Texas. You can see his work and more at www. KaijuPoet.com

More Books from John Baltisberger

www.ingramcontent.com/pod-product-compliance
Lightning Source LLC
Chambersburg PA
CBHW031251210726